# hungree throat

## BRITISH COLUMBIA
## ARTS COUNCIL
An agency of the Province of British Columbia

*Compliments of the BC Arts Council,
an agency of the province of British Columbia*

# bill bissett

# hungree throat

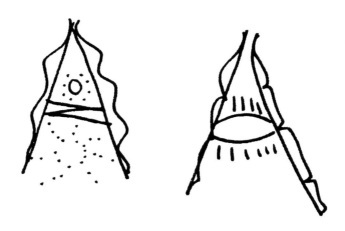

*a novel in meditaysyun*

TALONBOOKS

© 2013 by bill bissett

Talonbooks
P.O. Box 2076, Vancouver, British Columbia, Canada V6B 3S3
www.talonbooks.com

Typeset in Arial and printed and bound in Canada
Printed on 100% post-consumer recycled paper

First printing: 2013

The publisher gratefully acknowledges the financial support of the Canada
Council for the Arts, the Government of Canada through the Canada Book
Fund, and the Province of British Columbia through the British Columbia Arts
Council and the Book Publishing Tax Credit for our publishing activities.

Library and Archives Canada Cataloguing in Publication

Bissett, Bill, 1939–
        Hungree throat / Bill Bissett.

Issued also in electronic format.
ISBN 978-0-88922-745-3

        I. Title.

PS8503.I78H86 2013        C813'.54        C2013-900150-6

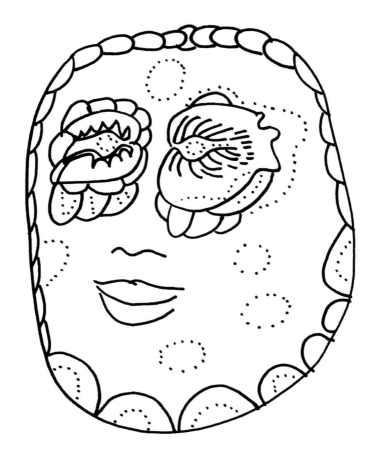

thanks 2 duncan horner 4 th front covr photgraph
n 2 jordan stone 4 front n back covr design n 4 xcellent
frendship & 2 carl peters 4 his book on my work –
textual vishyuns & 2 michael cobb 4 back covr pix
n lenore coutts 4 scanning uv back cover ptg & 2 yo
yo meow my mothr joys cat 4 sew veree guiding insites
& thanks 2 workman arts wher i have bin th poet in residens
09–13  n 2 th secret handshake & speshul thanks 2
karl siegler 4 editing & 2 christy siegler 4 mor copee
editing & all lay out and wrap up work 4 hungree throat
& 2 shane nagel – shane@massmediainc.ca
n 2 pete dako  4 our recent cd "nothing will hurt" n
2 b releesd in 2013 "hungree throat"

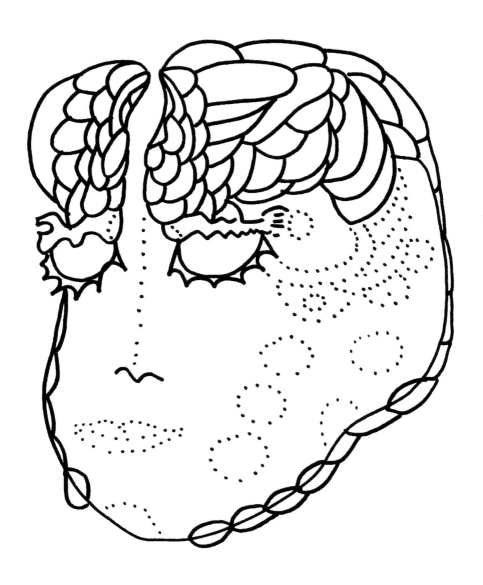

"... the mind is its own place and in itself can make a heaven of hell, a hell of heaven ..." john milton

## introduction 2 brian   freedom in re sisting a routeen  resetting th rue

tai chi  evree morning n meditating uplifts
accepting th heeling routeen can b liberating

i did sumthing but eye 4get what i did
i did sumthing but eye remembr what i did
i did sumthing i know n just now i 4get
what i did  i got past what i did n now ium
dewing sumthing  what i did n what u did
timez 10  i did sumthing n just now i remembr
 what i did n  i just now i know i did membr re
 what it was  th bodee likes routeen remembr
 n change   both ar inevitabul   olay  th first
narrativ may b th digestiv system  n time n haute
n remedee  n melodee  n atonal n dissonans n
 letting go  th memoree   shaking th hed


 thats all i can say 4 now  thats all i can say now
 thats all i can say 4 now  moovments uv luck

ium gonna cook th stove  oxidate th wounds
deep breething in2 them  sending th oxygen in
n make soup is all  will it work that way  say
yu  i have plans 4 ths 2day yu can say theyr
not much but theyr my plans  lay ovr  say

9

tai chi n meditaysyun  uplift bettr thn
aneething  stedeez heart rate n bodee
agilitee  nothings fool proof   all ths just
2 get redee 2 go swimming  n find wun
self  all th neurons  n motor fakulteez
meshing  n knitting 2gethr   n 2 go 2 work
at davisville n yonge yu say    hmmmm
sew bizaar  davisville n yonge  thats sew
specifik  its a trampoleen  uv his thin king
ar we nevr not konnektid
life is sew strange n
wintr is heer agen
why why why why why why why why
sumtimez disembodeed  n figurs in th filigree
voices reign ovr our physikal   tapestree we cant
intensyuns lost              climb out uv  dash
seeminglee n sniplets uv       or run 2 ground  sky
narrativ may haunt us         moon  stedee th taybul
as we redee 4 anothr flite  fraysr vallee          glows
canyun song  hells gate n th loamee medow        we
ar inside
dayze go  wher dew they go  th sun     until weer not
goez  we know wher it goez  th        grows
rainbow floating ovr th mountain          groans
how manee suns  how manee dayze      n fade
sunshine changing 2 brite nite
stringing stars  stars on a string


me n th tigr  running til spring
apeer on a clff edge  looking out at th
see  how manee suns  how manee seez
how manee branches uv th soul reeching
2 grow  purpul hills  blu rocks  great brown

10

buffalo lying down  watr falls from its
red eyes  a thousand pine treez make
up its hair
dayze go  wher dew they go  we onlee can touch
theyr strange memoree  see th eagul is laffing
out ther  above th rapids  laffing with me  n th
tigr  soaring sew hi in our dreems

we hope 2 take th voyage uv th dreemrs  past
sand n medow  past ocean n stars  past
spinning moonbeems  past pluto n mars
sevn voices whispring    sevn voices telling
me n th tigr  sailing 2 th   end   me n th tigr
sailing until th end  uv aneewher  look at it
glow  hoping 4 time  blowin 4 love

whos waiting 4 us at th  end uv th road
whos waitin 4 us at th  end uv th road
whos waiting 4 us at th  end uv th road
whos waitin 4 us at th  end uv th road
whos cum 2 meet us   at th top uv th hill
whos walkin with us   thru th mountain
whos walkin with  us  thru th rainbow
whos walkin with us  thru th storm

dayze go   wher dew they go  dayze go
wher dew they go

stringing stars    stars on a string
stringing stars     stars on a string

# brian

th idea uv brian  6 ft brown hair  grey eyez  alwayze
on th verge uv getting in shape  nevr qwite getting ther
reelee living with an invisibul prson or ideaz n sumtimez
daring 2 live by himself reelee  yu will surround yrself
with acoutrements  his fathr sd 2 him enuff timez it
was almost a permanent memoree  a prophesee  a curs
mantra  an ordr  command  what duz a child heer  2 b
chagrind admonishd  2 let go  2 pass on  who recalls
what  but himself  lankee n hot  waiting in th foyer uv
his life   yu will eet a peck uv dirt b4 yr twice marreed
his mothr sd 2 him singing rocking back n forth with
him in her arms   pushing back his cutikuls sew th half
moons on his nails cud fullee show  now isint that bettr

brian himself  diffrent 4 evreewun n 4 himself  brian
himself  outside uv kontext  we live out our dramas
dreems with what we thot think uv ourselvs  evree
wuns diagrams n condishyunal paradigms  his not
sew espeshulee  he wunderd a lot  was he reelee
living his own life  th life he wantid  is wanting  did
want  or a life he put 2gethr uv all th amalgams uv
konsciousness  n feeling th beautee uv sew much
reelee n uv sew manee he cud oftn feel th cello now
deep within n how unkritikalee n gratefulee sentimen
tal in th best sens he was bcumming   was that it tho
he liked 2 work n his boy frend wud cum evree three
dayze or four n they wud get it on  but wud his work
draw on ths   evenshulee what if ther wer no struggul
within  no fighting 4 anee prmissyun  what if it wer
alredee grantid n ther was onlee 2 enjoy   nevrthless

how deer evreething was   bcumming   n how horrifik
in th world  whn wasint it did int lessn th  horror he
felt sew manee powr peopul  left sew  much hurt n
disapointment in theyr wake  th shock  uv it  n th sew
veree oftn th beautee uv it   th life  n th  wundr  n th
mirakul uv it  th brain keeps  on changing  th bartok
string quartet yeers all that   sew manee  prsons we ar
how sumptuous it all is sum  timez he thot touching th
taybul n rising n walking thr  u th furnitur  touch th win
dow 2 look out  sumtimes  a lot hurts  tho its nevr reelee
evreething th snow cum   ming agen its an old qwestyun
how much dew we make   ourselvs  our projeksyuns  n
evreewun elsus thr how   much ar circumstances byond
our kontrol  n predikting   is evreething what we choos
or ar th kontexts we entr   choises how he was still thrilld
with ths wun prson  cud   he reelee see himself as singul
that is   not living  with anee wun   tho in his aerial flites at
nite  merging 4 sure  definit  or was it th thrill uv th words
taking  place space  on th papr  how manee millyuns uv
yeers 2 get ther  n his veree tiny place in it   n th evree
thing    brian   milyuns uv yeers old   we all ar

n evn tho it sumtimez feels   now n is  each moment is
also ancient  accepting n  battuling his own   was it his
own  things make him cry  sumtimez now  th cheemo
whatevr how he lovd dew  ing sew much uv what he was
dewing n with enuff xercise  he still cud  still look 4ward
2 each possibilitee   brite morning  2 look out in amayze
ment  adoraysyun  gratefulness   whats fair got 2 dew
with it   give n yu will maybe  reseev  not ther but sum
wher  n he was now undetektabul n grateful   ahhh

brian  his frend howard sd 2 him   cumming in brians
small apartment ovrlooking th mountains   n th erth
worlds largest innr citee park  yu ar such a prson uv
nostalgia   no ium not reelee brian sd  its great 2 see

13

yu n hold yu like ths  we cud b aneewher  our kontext
is what we make it  we cud b at th foot uv mont royal
th plateau  or in venice  remembr how that was  or no
a nu place  fresh citee  nu citee  ocean or lake or moun
tain or 4est  air mooving th curtains inside n its not yet
evn that kold  on our mouths n hungree throats finding
relees taste n  look  my hand  th feelings returnd 2 my
fingrs  my bionik eyez   we find ourselvs in all thees
moovs  our notaysyuns notes   all our selvs  can we feed
n maintain thees selvs we  wer reelee waiting 4 us  our
selvs  surelee we ar thees  fragments mooving thru th
fragments  appuls n sub  mareens laundree n th full moon
strange  crashes  sounds   in th nite  n at last giving up
agen th strange mythologizd  seeming autonomee uv th
singul life  opn th balconee n  lets go 2 bed agen  all th
peopul huddul 2gethr  cuddul    trace each othrs disa
peering ribs n spine  its not 4   kriticism or teeching its
4 finding th wayze 2 play n   accept each othrs strivings
all what we get up 4  lay   down with  all ths talking  oh
yes brian sd  his fingrs   navigating his life on howards
back

thank yu xcellent brian sd   whispring 2 th breething  th
galaxee n in2 howard n they  both startid laffing as th
snow moovd in2 th living room   ther was no rush 2 close
th balconee door  it was that  erlee yet in th wintr  brian
n howard wer each off th road  n inside each othr  it did
int mattr eithr yet 4 how long

       latr in th nite brian got up  n rememberd  whn rosalee
       saw him off at th bus going  north  in anothr countree
       he sd he felt like he was going  in2 th unknown n she
       sd 2 him we alwayze ar brian   he felt th wundr n re
       turnd 2 bed  with howard

scape scope

aabbbbbbbbbbbbbbbb

uuuuuuuuOommmm

wwwwwwweeeeeeee00

.........iiiiiii.i.i.i.i.0,o.i

15

## now what

brians big idea  that we dont have as much 2 dew
with wher we ar as we think   that translating an
alredee translatid idea n that its implikaysyuns  re
free will an eureka idea gives us stratajee  lives
n sew on  intensyunaliteez n acceptans n subms
yuns blah blah ar fr sure nothing nu n if he gives
up on ths pursuit 2 undrstand  2 reklaim his tra
jektoreed  moovment thru all ths time n space
how 2 get mor self realizing    ackshulizing  or
reelee present   2 find what he was wanting  th
companee  sex  partnr  paintr  less alone  mor
time  mor innr health regardless  what was it  yu
want frends  take ystrday 4 instans  a prfekt day
n nite  evree day cud b ripe 4 all that  n why not
now wer heer  n th memoreez juxtaposing with
th line  lines  uv th present s  sumtimez a hevee
moteef influensing our awareness wareeness
or boldness  dpending on what seeminglee
random memoree it is  whethr its eye can dew
ths  or what am i waiting 4  look at th last time
th last line  n th alwayze xcuse uv work 2 dew
that yu love eeting th present prsonal views or
is it th same diffrens  like they usd 2 say

16

# life is strange

challenging  fr sure  oftn sew full uv pain  n oftn as
well   filld with beautiful moments  pleysyurs  that
transform us 2 nu undrstandings  n we can go 4 an
othr round  get anothr kik at th can  get our second
wind  n sumthings cum up in th nu mist fog morning
is it us  walking 2ward ourselvs  dropping in  saying
hello in th midst uv our sleep routeen  howard was
wundring abt all ths  dew we split from our bodee
selvs  as in astral travl  part uv us goez out 4 a whil
out uv erths lattitude evn  n th othr part stays at
home minding th store   ar we oftn diskonnekting
with ourselvs  have sum adventurs whil th othr
parts ar growing  dewing things  lerning nu skills
cumming back 2 us ovr th hill horizon sew happee
2 b cumming home agen  2 th familyar

brian was musing on all thees apertures n storeez
approaches 2 th strangeness uv being whil he was
working at th galleree wher he did filing phoning
hanging  selling  n talking with evreewun who wud
cum in  if they wer wanting 2 talk  a gud day was
xcellent peopul n xcellent conversaysyuns  leeding
sub textualee 2 a possibul sale  that wud get referrd
2  that wud give hope  or an xcellent n reel sale  that
wud afford reel hope n part uv th maintanens  sum
dayze it was difikult 2 conjure up all that  othr dayze
it was fine  latelee no sales  no hints  no jestyurs

## wher ar th art buyrs

who ar th art buyrs  why
wher dew they hang  why  why

ar they phoning in
ar they planning 2 cum n find
th veree great art from ths galleree
ium waiting  ium waiting
ar th art buyrs cumming soon
                              soon
ar th art buyrs
hiding  in remors  from loving art
2 much  thees prices ar reelee
resonabul   slashd

wher can i find th art buyrs
employing strange ruses
n countr fuses  subtr fugues
all thees derivativs  fuses n
fugues  trying sew hard not
                2 b diskoverd

dew th art buyrs want my dna
will they frame me
hang me  is it mor safe
2 not look 4 them   wher ar
th art buyrs  hiding

ar th art buyrs bcumming 2 conservativ
thers no munee in conservatism
wher ar th art buyrs putting theyr
munee   artists
need theyr munee

how cud th art buyrs have enuff art alredee
did i take a wrong turn
ar they deliberatelee
avoiding me

how cud aneewun have enuff art  beautee
TREWTH

if they want art
but dont have th time 2 get in2 th galleree
they cud send munee in  n we th artists
cud ship  art 2 them  save them a trip
give them a dreem  what they want

ar th art buyrs at home  watching teevee
afrayd  afrayd 2 spend   have they spent it
all

what if we refuse 2 dew art  oh ok that
wunt work  eye see  we must keep on
dewing art  4 nothing  sew they can
buy us  aftr wev gone

n our work  can b in a vault

n no wun can see it

dont worree  its all

gud

=] in th midst uv my||||
unee's
i was nevr what
yu wantid     i cud
nevr pleez enuff=
wi||a||   cud

# sumtimez brian lookd back 4 sum

guidans  how he got thru ths how he got thru
that  miseree or back up against th wall predik
ament  keep a gud sens uv humour  nothing is th
end uv th world  sept th akshul end uv th world
waiting on th funding will it cum thru  n whn  n
th eeree fateeg that results in th waiting 2 heer
n not being abul 2 think aneemor uv evn anothr
opsyun  thats th art galleree game  its anothr
day  opn up th store  have hi hopes  get th koffee
going  cope with th depressyun  beleev sumthing
great  gud  uplifting can happn  start n welkum th
nu day  get th lites on  turn up th heet its wintr
aftr all  i love it heer  its sew beautiful brian sighd
in a dreem   how 2 save th dreem

whats anothr funding sources bsides whats happend
n whats with th soshul agensee  wch 2 him rite
now feels like theyr playing him 4 a fool  tho its
reelee in theyr own way they ar trying 2 help  not
returning calls  gess thers nothing 2 say  yet  as
whn 2 pick up th chek  try n stay yu know optimistik
th art galleree life is th strangest  aneething in th art
industreez is sew strange  aneething can happn  if
yu can live with aneething as yr dailee diet yr ok  yr
in th circus world now  alwayze have bin  peopul
undr valu art but use it 4 evreething in theyr lives
all th time  they undrvalu it sew they dont have 2
pay 4 it  n yu remembr all th remarkabul help that

happns yu keep working  peopul dew cum 2 th rescue
thers no job securitee  not in th art bizness  n peopul
individuals  group cum tord yu  out from th shadows
n bring yu munee  opportunitee  help yu cud nevr have
4 seen  imagind  th sources  its also th surprize bizness

th big tent can go down  or up  at a moments notis n
yu can live with that  but all th time  well dont hang yr
self yet  sumwun will cum in n buy a work they reelee
love n it can set yu up 4 a month  like we can live 4
evr  stay groundid  oh ok  keep bizee with th phoning
how did ths happn    wher is evreething  breething in
th danforth

cumming home at nite   now surreelee  aftr closing up
th galleree  it had bin a   reelee gud day  it was veree
inkee  evreething  no moon   they had sold a small ptg
veree speshul wun n a promise  uv a big wun selling  or
wuns latr in th month  feeling bettr  he cud see th lites
in th buildings but maybe not th  buildings  th lites yes
ran in2 howard on his way in2 his  building  howard had
bin waiting 4 him out ther in all th  snow n dark nite cold
n aura  they huggd n  went in   in th  lobbee  in th ele
vator in th hall along or down th  hall  get th keys  out
in th door  opn th door  in th  apartment  hall close th
door   throw theyr clothes on th  floor  bed n fuck theyr
brains out

## sew what ar yu gonna dew now howard

askd brian  let go  as much as i can  brian sd n
b as optimistik as possibul  n dew as littul as
possibul  2 validate  th stress n th depressyun
cawsd by th suspens uv povrtee    dew self
care  find  sum benefisent blessing within time

in a societee sew dedikatid 2 kontrol uv evree
thing  arint peopul entituld 2 at leest ths  out
side uv th damnd work ethik  kontrolling n th
societal templates  kontrolling evreething els
can thees dynamiks kontrol evn who fucks whom

omg  th phone call came  it came in  they have
enuff 4 three months  now  th granting prson
was veree wundrful n heartfelt  brian was rekovr
ing his enerjee 4 othr things n sew rock on sew
amayzing  that help can cum

brian was givn 2 undrstand  tho that th responsibil
itee 4 munee n evreething like that wud b givn ovr 2
th agensee he had alwayze undrstood that  but not
that it wud b 4 such a small amount  tho essenshul
n totalee needid  n flow thru 4 rent wud not b on time
as he had alwayze made it   sew he wud still need 2
borrow    mor angst 2 let go uv wher  wud he b  wher
it wud mattr  reelee mattr  most probablee reelee
that wud b with his own work  painting n starting
agen 2 grow in2 his own life  a turtul pulling it self
in2 its own shell  if possibul growing away from anee
kodependenseez   how can we make sum wun els
responsibul 4 us  as apeeling as that is can b  or what
dew we dew whn sum wun wants us 2 b responsibul
4 them  n blame us if we dont want 2 dew 4 them  n
they yell at us   run away  run away  that can work  no
blaming  intraktiv  tensyun weul  feel guiltee 4  get yr
own stuff dun   run  run  skip  n run th remedeez ar
all sew various  konflikting n  oftn ineffektiv  peopul
cant get us  its 2 late or not  enuff   thees ar not onlee
meditaysyuns  musings  or qwestyuns  theyr molekular
organik  visceral  reelee  letting go  is it yu can think
up sum disturbing passyuns posishyuns  fragments
dont hag out abt it   th graveyard we ar all mooving
thru   evn tho ther ar sew manee times uv awesum
ness  uv byond byond  uv sweetness  brillyans giving
transcendens  still we ar all oomd with a d   as we
subskribe 2 evolushyun  its worth it 2 get bettr  all uv
us  get th canvas on th easul  chill  get it redee n 2
gethr  n rest  yu wer sick now yr bettr  howard is
cumming  try not 2 relive th late 90s brian ok he

sd 2 himself  xercising n waiting 4 th paint 2 dry  2
get startid  agen  whos vois is ths  building n letting
go  thats it  yes  th fateeg aftr th grueling suspens n
thats lifting now  sew b kool  we can work 2 build

we dont take it with us   rashyunal prspektivs  we ar all
deeplee involvd in ths  process  in ths life n deth cycul ths
dsintegraysyun  ovr wch  we reelee dew have no kontrol
letting go n still being  involvd in sum aspekts uv it  like
letting go uv a great love  th love is  within th decisyuns
wher 2 place my bodee  wher 2 p lace my bodee being is
within me  n i return th favors i can n want 2   th grand
childrn uv sum great  mewsik ar th maybe  last wuns 2
reinakt it thru th magikul  chiarascuro uv time  n th piano
making th melodees seem  beethoven  bach  gershwin
arlen  weill  elington  strayhorn  tatum  mcpartland  sew
manee  labyrithean thru th halls  antee rooms  meeting
rooms  dens  going thru th hall wayze th mewsik uv sew
manee yeers  genres supporting us as we go  sumthing
sumwun  2  hold  dissolvs  is  flesh 4 a  whil  stairwayze
erode  dissolv  wayze in2 th heart murray houston jackson
also n grow strongr  making th  melodeez seem inevitabul
roach holiday peterson   bartok  n from  almost god  that
is peopul at  theyr best  can help each othr   doktor dre
walking by a  crowdid  happee loud  restaurant adele  a
cry 4 love  rollin in  th deep  30 below th  ice wind  craks
at yr skin

  brian n howard first met at such a place  gathring  they
saw each othr n each mor feeling fullee alive thn they had
evr bin  as if all had bin onlee ghostlee n unwarrantid b4
whn they wer introdusd  sumwun was playing  sumwun 2
live 4  by billy strayhorn  yu know it was impossibul yet

it reelee playd that way n they bcame instantlee inseprabul
that was 4 yeers ago now  almost 5  ths was mor thn th
science ficksyun flash   that was gratefulee ther but evree
thing els flowd thru n from th inishul neurologikal kreetshur
instant recognishyun   evn if they had bin sew close b4
thos fleeting nites in madagaskar onlee 2 let go  n now
find agen

        th buzzr rings  its howard  xcellent  peopuls
        konflikts ar all abt letting go  easier sd thn
        dun   how much th ko dependeneez  th see
saws  if yu dew ths  why cant yu undrstand me  can yu
help me  let go  oh i know i can dew ths all by myself  n
moov on totalee  i reelee dew want mor uv a prsonal
life n heer he is   thank god  if ther is wun   both and  n
whethr th nitemare  boneyard  memoreez  scarrd organs
th bodeez n ashes piling up  we still can glide thru thees
vishyuns  dewing what we can  came 2  intrakt  abt n help
out n in  its howard  n brian n howard get it on  th sun
going   mor n mor until total darkness covrs th playground
uv theyr lives  they chill 4 anothr nite   sigh  cum   let go
remembr th fluiditeez  th word no can bcum yes n yes can
bcum no   or diffrentlee put in2 acksyun  thos instances
startid  keep going with th damages n bandages n th
changes  ther reelee dusint need 2 b a constant aneething
tho we may want it 2 b  it  is its own thing  willful  petulant
n sew much randomness  n onlee sumtimes what we want
                                         smiles
is it 2 b in touch with mor thn what we want  sumtimez th
importans uv our selvs plays on in othr realms uv our e
ternal in th moment devosyuns   dew yu follow me howard
brian askd  sure howard sd putting down his pliers  sure
altho i did undrstand it bettr ystrday  i still get it   ther ar
manee realms uv consciousness   ther ar now three times
as manee peopul on erth as ther wer in 1950

# running  pushing against th wind heeving yr

bodee against th akreesyun uv karma that like as
not makes yu  or cud make yu  if yu wer 2 allow it
sit down  give up  but thrusting yr bodee 4ward  up
up  against th inert seeming obdurate willfulness  up
th hill furthr furthr up still a wayze 2 go  yul get ther
sheesh  its decembr  th top uv th hill  wher th rest n
fire warmth wud b  is  th top uv th hill uv th yeer  its
a wayze yet  duz th top make itself sew continualee
out uv reech  teeching us all what  that its a hard
road  or its a veree steep hill  humblee weul get ther
if nowun pushes against us  n without protest a bettr
day may cum without fricksyun  or daunting heights
on wch spred out n upward is th onlee pathway othr
thn teleportaysyun or levitaysyun  my nose hurts  th
bone uv it  from th verbal mental fight i was in ystr
day othr thn that n th weeriness from sum uv th
anguls uv th angels  sumtimes what theyr up 2  con
versaysyun uv cross purposes  cinderellas twistid
sistrs  n th wethr  th disapointments  trying 2 recall
remembr th ekstaseez th inkredibul pleysurs n
loyalteez  th brillyant frend ships  keep goin  th top
uv th hill th end uv th yeer  th dayze ar getting longr
agen  th end uv th steep inkline is in site  brian thot
onlee a few mor kilometrs 2 go  go thru th fateeg
dont stop  now getting past ths hard part  bad mem
or eez  all th attacks  th transgressyuns  as we try 2
get past all thees  thots thots  grabbing a solid looking
branch 2 hold on 2  2 pull us ovr a diffikult bump  n al
most flounderd yet keep on  soon  wunt ther b mor lite
n rest at th top  wuns we get ther  n wud not evreething
wudint it b alrite with howard n work n his calmness

acheevd at last  not getting interferrd with  by a secret
lee angree n jealous rival  who had bin a frend  life sew
changes

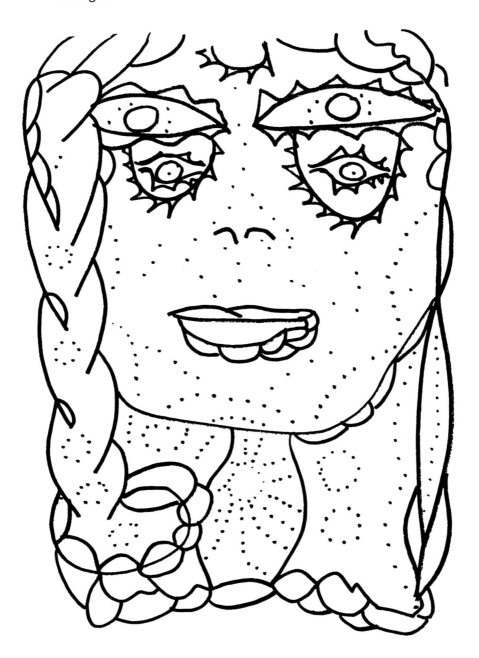

# rival 4 what

what if thers no resolushyun  all teer drenchd  or a
happeeness bound  a 4evr konnekting ending  what is
that that dusint end  yu ar immediatelee luckee  in
krediblee  i dont need a moral i need an oral  or not all
dont drink th bittr t uv being alone  enjoy th time  how
evr it is  nevr 2 long at a time aneething  each day is
still a mirakul n on a swinging branch now  ths will
hold yu until it dusint  sumwun 2 touch who dusint
want 2 use yu   will choos yu  th odds ar etsetera who
cares last try  i felt myself walking away in th crowdid
food court reelee walking away n thn eye reelee cudint
n walkd back at an undrstanding i knew he reelee
reelee did not want 2 leev me eithr  with us both evr
we returnd 2 th taybul 2 negosheeate mor  i cud onlee
say no abt th mattr at hand  th beleef n shared use uv
langwage n wud he 4give me 4 akshulee helping him
ths meens ths  that sz that  duz my happeeness reside in
onlee how othrs intrpret events   th third prson was make
ing 2 manee nagging n negativ inroads in 2 my frends n
my life his verbal abuse had 2 b stoppd  it was 2 late 4
diplomasee  i i i i i i  u u u u u  h h he  he he he  she  she
she  all ths hurtful n boring atempts at dominans in th
jousting  th politiks  why  whn evreething is possibul
cudint we all bring 4 that  ther  bye bye bye  ther ther
yu step out uv  oh well  oh milk uv human kindness
sumtimes it dusint serv veree well  sumtimes it reelee duz

wud he lose his reel frend in all ths  brian prayd  it was
howard at th door  n now he felt he had 2 get it on  4 th
reassurans  n th self esteem  yu step 4 ths whil out uv th
stressd puzzul  wun swoon n thru th blush goez on n
startuls eyez mouth breth find each othr breth b letting
each out uv us  out uv our puzzul traps n moov   its not

like going with th best lovr evr n nevr seeing agen   get
up b4 he wakes up  get my clothes on n walk out n walk
no idea uv how 2 return ther evn no end 2 all that  what if
thers no resolushyun byond th moment all teer drenchd
or happeeness bound a 4evr konnekting self korrekting
ending  nevr known

jestures from th 3rd floor windo w did sustain me he addid softlee as in a treetop on humming birds

# smashd  an eye in th hand

i dont want 2 evr get attachd 2 aneething that
moovs he sd agen  solar an eye in th wind  waving
n waving  th vines twirling round  my bodee  rising
lifting bcumming th tarot uv th world  now i see it
hold it up  its me on th card red pyramid blu flames
mor show  its not  its motor onlee n th drilling nevr
th vois thats yu  its th vois that can happn thru yu
n now yr caut in th middul th serving prson sd yes
i sd  i hope it gets bettr she sd  did yu heer that i
askd my frend  i herd he sd   th flying horses at
yuunyun staysyun ar ridrless n all th hands fingrs
clutching on  th nails ripping off  skraper teez
th skidding uv tock  try 2 hold on th sides uv th
strait uv canso n th cabot trail  not th apokolips
not th pegasus x 4

theyr riding hi ovr our heds  like our dreems sumtimes
ar on th cloud emisyuns uv our lives  lites as mooving
our puzzuls btween th lines uv th parametrs bordrs
goin off 2 northrn boundaree school agen establishd
suggestid by  wch committee as we rock on th evo
lushyunaree thrust  dont we all want 2 b part uv  call
th frostid ombudsman coz th bids buds birds arint
cumming out quiklee enuff in th bettr buttr cyclone
sew manee ded alredee  hold on 2 yr toe nails  thos
peopul ar great 4 art ichokes n sweet sardeens lettr
uv appul starts with an a  banana starts with a b  th
change uv seismik nervusness it was odd reelee whn
she sd she had bin abusd in her last relaysyunship as
we all regardless uv how much we liked her saw her
as veree kontrolling  maybe thats it tho  how it can
happn o th myths we can tell abt ourselvs n evreewun
els yet isint that what wud  cud  reelee happn  eye thot
who thot yu thot  n thinking  elektrik sir cut tree that

## thinking resin ateing th stedee murmurs uv trans mittr drones dreems

control n get abused that from thn on yu want 2
take sum control if yu can  that getting victimizd
cud nevr happn agen  well it was a nu day n we
wer a bit anxious abt hypotheses n wch way 2
flew who n saw th remains rewinds reminding in
an ivoree glayze padduld n garnishd in th harrowd
sheet n th easul was waiting  n th motor cycul was
waiting  n th skript was waiting n th camera n reme
mber th qwark xpress n th lovr in th secret place n it
was a nu day  get enuff sugar n salt  just enuff  not 2
much  remembring all thos great timez in ambrosia
anaxoreeaa  how wasint it sew great ther n sew rock
on margareeta cap rev in compensaysyun  2 eleph
ants in love  yes yes yes  ium heer bside yu  alwayze
uv kours unkul switzerland  dew yu want 2 cum 4 t
ium sorree i cant cum 2nite  ium not allowd out 2nite
th gods n goddesses n th veree tall prsonabul prison
guards  will not allow me 2 go out  yu havint bcum
unavailabul yet have yu no  2morro ok  oh ok take
care ok nite nite  take care  maybe its nite  maybe
its O  three elephants in love  yes maybe its 5 ele
phants  ium sew grateful 4 ths moment emnu evn
tho thers no wun 2 talk 2 air port chilis ium just an
elephant in love in an airport yr neithr heer nor ther
yet yu ar heer n ther also  who seez yu ther  heer
how important is that  th witnesses its a top down
day  in th merree go round  its a top down day what
evr yu say  th wind th wind  in th sun feel th warmth
in th sun  first time evr  n its almost may  wow its a
top down day n we can go out n play  th warm in
our minds  we drive thru th see  all th peopul happee
ness in reech  a thousand towrs  stand b4 us  we

cannot climb them all  tuesday may 26th 11:45 am  th
othr side uv wher  its not as untrew as yu wud think it
is 6 months  in 5 months slite dry mouth a smile regard
less saliva balans singing breething anxietee balans
thru deep breething  almost all ther n trust in being
evn tho i have no idea wher i am  proof reed on th lava
plane  how manee times have i dun a few things  yu
didint want 2 n in th long run yu benefitid  or going
highr up  th hill 2 th place uv unlerning  a silvree skaree
day  how dew yu know what line is veree realistik at
all  uninteresting  like yu would find sum wun elsus
work in yr own or if we give up wanting 2 control  th
present or th outcum  how we can get paranoid  n as
they say no gud deed goez unpunishd    what nothing
duz it reelee all signify  skard uv each othr  realizing
all th help we ar alredee getting  n sing th heeling time
th ride 2 th palace  th strawberee palace  th 38 inches
give give let give give let let give ve ve ve eva  evi  i
think ium sure i think ium sure je pense i love linguistik
improbabiliteez  write abt pine n write abt mogan n dont
tell  n make a pickshur uv ther hous  western imperial
megalomania  1 clairvoyant  4 duplex just accounts  out
uv th bridgeweer  th torrents n tumult th ipplong 4 sum
advantage sway powr its sew pathetik sad our attrak
syuns get in2 such messes  thers nothing 2 moralize
love  leeds 2 love  all th great adventures we xperiensd
n reelee recentlee ruefulee  th honourabul behaviours
n sumtimes verbal abuse runs n ruins it all amount #
17  n unit # 7  bathos getaway  4 blks off commershul
white hous walk south past 4 blu garbage cans woodn

gate  4 sets uv lips  i cud have gone byond th home
byond  th hous saying cud b sew grateful 4 th time
n sew gasping 4 watr  august 17  nineteen 89  at last
i got faxd  in th turning bliss uv th tidal town  i cud
have gone thru evreewher  who cudint have  fate n
th parlour bowling games timez three thousand infint
lee evree wher  thru cellophane doorwayze saying
saying watr watr i can b faithful in a littul mor inde
pendent town neer thos falls  thats wher i cud b all
things  yes  ths is delishyus  isint it  i love thees
taste buds  still with me he sd   evn whn yu protekt
a lovd wun in or a place yu can onlee hurt yr self as
well if othrs push that hard 4 powr can they get theyr
feelings hurt as if they wer gud peopul  what dew
peopul who bhave badlee reelee dew whn theyr  by
them selvs  dew they evr feel sorree  dew they self
justify n onlee what 2 get what they want that they
ar unaware uv what els is going on  othr peopuls
hurt feelings   whn love is damaged it evenshulee
can onlee go  n that in a painful way  dew they feel
th pain they engendr  cawse  is thr anee prcentage
in going ther  why not let it go  yu cant figur  why
not let it go  but can yu lern  can yu  what n wher
is th bottom line  why dew yu fall 4 such diffikult
n hard choises  cases  in othrs n in yrself  can yu
reflekt deepr  can yu run away agen  agen  thers
sew much stuff  committments  things yu want 2
dew  wher  heer  th peopul yu leev n leev yu agen
looking 4 th resiprositee yu take care uv sumwun
n they in theyr wayze yu  n thn they turn on yu  all

yu want 2 dew is 2 protekt  sum wun  sum place n
not falling 4 evreething  if yu hadint bin abusd whn yu
wer young cud yu tell bettr discern distinguish evn th
stuffd birds in th windows n th large dolls in th gardn
lookd askanse as he walkd by aneewun wud reseev
that treetment  tho he almost tuk it prsonalee  in th
fiers april winds  wun uv th dolls was tottering almost
falling ovr  knocking against th walls uv th sand box sum
uv its robins egg blu paint cum off on2 th raven haird
doll  try not 2 get lost in yr interior uv doubt n confuse
yun n or being  th victim uv aneewun elsus crueltee
try n stay up evn tho nothing may happn aneemor  th
setting  th land n treez  erth sky  ar beautiful  th myst
ereez uv evreething  litr non combatativ wayze 2 see
n undrstand evreething  if possibul  that wud take his
mind off aneething terribul that has happend  try 2
remembr th gud stuff  not denial  but awareness that
wundrful things have n dew happn  n how yu can take
yr mind off thos ghosts  yrself  dewin it yrself  protekt
yrself n yr work  each day n each nite  what yu did n
dew 4   scrubbing th floors  working n watching  a great
moovee  not sew hard  in a beautiful milieu  tho it onlee
touches yr soul n being  not yr proaktiv prson  yu dont
evr have evreething  we have sum parts partlee  parts
uv speech each a hand in th mirror  sumtimez th seekr
mirror melts  sumtimez we hurt each othr veree much n
try  try  2 start agen    or can we cum back from that now
did we go 2 far   th jelousees hurt n manipulaysyuns 2
out in th opn now 2 heel unstuff enuff   or as sum wun
wuns sd  love is not alwayze loving

# its a veree ovrcast nite brian sighd oh

hoping howard wud cum n he cud put away
all th past claims n countr claimings  button
button  whos got th button  how we gobbul
at each othr  whn yu re entr th room  wch
objekts on th taybul ar missing  what dew yu
remembr  recall  diamonds n brik a brak  2
tortoises  a pees uv mango  n bandages at th
redee  as they usd 2 say shrieking  striking
slashing flesh off  each othr  brian reelee needid
2 see things as potenshulee way much bettr
n bettr work on that  if its all dun with th mind
help 2 apees or help lift th nay sayrz n th basik
negativ feelings uv th powr kontrollrs  sew we
can all cum 2 th taybul n share fairlee  sew ar
thees just phases howevr unjust peopul go
thru  king n qween uv th kastul  th snow drifts
we theyr growing out uv what they find thers
no advantage ovr worth having as we dont
have aneething reelee   listn he sd  howard is
heer  ths is what i can dew  submit 2 whn it
is a levl uv playing field n not sum agonizing
n beautiful futile attachment  he was tirud uv
looking 4 unusalee gud looks beautee enchant
ment as it seems 2 bite  what was is it dpends
on th prson inside th mask howevr it is but how
dew yu see in  ah entrtainment  ah religyun ah
politiks n th natural disastrs  oh th evolushyun
aree thrust  hang on  if we can evolv with th

choices 2 us renewabul enerjee sources onlee
th air is healthier with less coal mines n burning
fossil fuel emisyuns less cancrs  less led in our
 lungs  its reelee qwite cleer  going in2 solar n
  wind   renewabul resources n hold on 2 each
 othr whn we what  can we dew all thos n no
obligaysyun   dewing it willinglee  n dewing self
        care we each have a reel rite 2    find
him n howard in bed finding th wayze 2gethr 2 b
2gethr 2 b 2gethr 4 at leest ths time n see what
happns  lonliness can leed 2 obsesyun slanting

things tord supposd wrongness rathr thn xcellens
n optimism make th calls  dont give in 2 or curtail
  yr aktiviteez 2 th tailoring uv th nay sayrs theyr
onlee peopul 2 like oh  like all uv us make th positiv
call oh th korrosiv naytur sumtimes uv relaysyun
ships evn espeshulee our organs cant take it all
thers sumthing 2 say  thers sumthing 2 say  yes
we impale ourselvs on our guts from th stress n
strain uv th 2 freqwent struggul  verbal abuse
n mind games   whos anee bettr  they bhave
badlee bcoz uv theyr insecuritees  can we help
them without getting hurt by them  send th lettr
loving it all  i meen joyfulee  yes  yes  n yes

# three salmon pomes *

## watching broadcast nus

i see th salmon talks will
        resume on monday

well thank god  at leest th
        salmon ar talking

\*  a symphony uv salmon was writtn in 2011 n at last ths trio uv
   salmon pomes  almost 12 yeers in th making bcame realizd

## speeking uv environmental issews

i dont think its fair uv peopul trying 2 stop
fish from farming  dew yu  why ar peopul

sew mad at say  salmon  farming  isint that
gud 4 th salmon  all th exercise in th work n

opn air  wunt farming make salmon strongr
mor agile  mor full uv nutrients  4 us 2
benefit  if peopul dont want 2 farm themselvs
aneemor  why not let salmon dew th farming

why stop  th salmon from farming  isint that
theyr decisyun 2 make  n wudint it b gud 4 all
konsernd

tho it cud b sd  how cud salmon farm on
theyr fins  2 push th ploughs etsetera  can
they bcum primates  ovrnite  n if not  can
they reelee farm on theyr backs  as sum
claim  can yu

imagine  salmon floundring  as sew manee
peopul have farmd on theyr backs  or was
that farming

## a symphony uv salmon

sibilant thru th up streem  swimming 4
    ward with dna fiersness  in th gold streem
  now  turning  green

unlike th salmon we can live longr thn giving
                                   birth
n cumming 2 th taybul  place all our magik
      objekts uv manee dimensyunal
                consciousness  on it

evn th taybul n all th objekts  we can place
    ther    glass figurines  wills  sacrid n
  arcane  cannistrs  uv kours  documentz
writtn agreementz  templates  emblems
                    narrativs
  uv our humours  laisons  n tragedeez
  th epoch  neurologikal  acuitee  our

  symphoneez  ar  mor  divers we think  we
  dont disapeer gradualee  among colours uv
    green  pink  gold  th pebbled  shore  em
    bedding  th fins  eyez n tails  n heds  n
  th inner  flanks  can we say  falling  falling
    in2 th erth  dissolving  in2 th wet ground

we disapeer in2 each othr  n our bones eez

in2 th erth  th fire  th vapour uv sumtimes
b4  also disapeering  iuv herd  we can heer
th symphony uv salmon  n th salmon singing
theyr liquid sibilants  songs n dreems
swimming  guiding us thru  in2

circuls  within circuls  sumtimes dizzeeing
within th rivr  running  upstreem  we all ar
evenshulee   rainbows  goldn  pink
evreething  salmon  n gorillas  all inside us

ther is no ending  2  bcumming

# self analysis

ok i have a penchent 4 obsessyun n worreeing  2 much
abt othrs 2 th point wher i cant find my own life  ium
generous n veree hard working  a gambler n dont kno
oftn how 2 take a day off  i 2 eezilee can see th negativ
side uv things   tho they ar oftn ther   n i work in my
brain 2 get 2 th up side  wch is also ther  n we dew
need 2 korrekt how othrs can try 2 dominate us  n try
not 2 take a long  gloom view  let all that go

yu ar 2 eezilee influensd in soshul n prsonal areas
that opsyun has bin placed ther as test  each rung on
th laddr  stairs  is filld with tests  n wher is th languor
nest  its not outside yu  tho things going well can
sure uv kours make yu feel bettr  is it wheels within
wheels  brian wunderd that  n self reflecksyun time

like yr fawlts turn in2 erasure n gifts 2 change xchange
all th chains made on us   we make on othrs 4 our climbs
above th obsessing sewrs n graveyards we like bosch
worldlee delites we live in  is marriage sum mutual claim
ing  we teer each othr apart if we dont satisfy each othr
we love each othr n seveerlee hurt each othr leeving
each othr alone  2 lick th wounds n sort it out  n let it
go n get ovr it  let it go  let it go  let it go  continuing 2

we can reelee nevr own aneewun n 4 sure equalee them
us  they pushd  out uv line  eye pushd back  it was an
othr test  based on memoree msundrstandings  gave me
huge migraine n mor time  alone  as if  punishment 4
being strong within  b flexibul  wher possibul n lerning
ther wer 2 women in th pool 2day  yelling with each othr

4 ovr an hour it was at first distrakting  terribul  i
kept on dewing mor laps  kept going  i had cum heer
wanting quiet  serenitee  letting th mental hurts go
insted thr was yelling  non stop  fine  i kept going
i had sd hi 2 them whn i had enterd th pool  they turnd
theyr backs  wun uv them had a child  who was
swimming in th low end  they had turnd theyr backs on
th child  it was byond strange   soon it felt like theyr
yelling was opera in th jakuzzi  publik private space
whats goin go  prson jumps in th pool  a sort uv box
dive   aftr a fast run tord th watr   drops from th air
splash in2 th watr  less thn half a metr away  i kept
on swimming  ium going 4 th 60 laps  whatevr  eye
wundr is evreewun whackd   in th food court ystrday
me n my best frend had a huge shoot out  can i tell
yu what happend  can i tell yu what happend  it was
wun uv th worst timez evr

why dew yu have 2 dfend yrself 2 sumwun yu love
n protekt th integritee uv yr joint ventur  n sand
wichd in ther is th knowing if they can say that n dew
that  evn they maybe cant help it  they dont love yu
or not aneemor  if they did  well erase that    its a bad
patch n yu bettr place yr feelings sumwher els  whats
keeping howard  whatul i dew  play ths out n gone
how long will th heart take 2 heel  n he was dfending
sum wun who was dissing me  i was paying atten
syun n protekting what wev built  konflikt  as he sd
latr i didint bow 2 his will  well i dont dew that  tho
i lovd ths prson n still dew  cum on 10 mor laps ok
ar snakes birds  clouds strings  work nothing  sure
categoreez dissolv  memoreez r taybuls  ar they
lites lamplit by windows  th shelving n lizards nite
goez up days fall n tree top monkeez glide n sew
manee uv th racoons ar giraffes n th memoreez will

evenshulee change us  it was like th magik flute theyr
voices cascading  papagano n papagana  i didint get
what i wantid  a sereen space n as it bcame fine n
helpd me mor  who duz  get what they want all th time
or evn enuff uv th time  n as it bcame fine  n helpd me
mor 2 let go  let it go is love  an illusyun  or 4 reel  why
dew we evr doubt ourselvs  lonliness  not enuff intr
acksyuns  work alone  not getting karessd enuff  n
attachment breeds sorrow n loss  getting it on without
attachment is protektiv but not love soonr thn latr but
evn celibate relaysyunships can hurt a lot   sumtimes
peopul dew meen streeking things  assholes  we cant
know  maybe theyv bin hurt sew they need 2 pass that
on n they dont know they dont know  that makes it
easier 2 4give n let go  chairs ar muskets  yu stood 4
sumthing n didint fall 4 aneethings  strawbereez ar
galaxeez th streek uv accusatoree meenings n finding
my own way 2 swim in th swimming baloons ar eye
lids th mascara laffing at sunrise th massacre uv th
embitterd weepee hillside poneez n felt pen petunias

wher ar they whn yu need them   brian got up  looks
around 4 howard  hes not in th bed  th bathroom  anee
wher hes gone  if hes 4givn evreething thats happend
b4  can he start agen  duz he need howard 2 get on
with his nu life  dewing ths nu thing  duz 4givness covr
th praktikal aps as self defens n that it wunt happn agen
uv kours it will  deranged growths uv th mind n spirit
start from ths  how we see things  can we intend  4 our
pleysyurs aftr th injureez n th attacks  pray 4 pees  love
n moov on  letting go   we dont adapt well  ar maladaptiv
n th tragedee is that it  cell rings  howard  sz he was losing
his courage  can they talk latr in th day  is ths yet anothr
game  or is he sinseer  how dew yu know aneemor  slap
stik manoeuvrs in th inkreesing dark  evreebodee loves
a parade  ar th floats reelee as xcellent as they usd 2 b

## deep threds   deep dreds

divers divors pomes  arint we all divrs  4 perls
  is it debussey  oystrs  n each othr  magik
  fish   di  vors  di      no  its bizet

  we live in a graveyard  we ar born in a grave
   yard  we evenshulee fall in2 th graveyard

  whil wer in it we try 2 improov th graveyard
   get kondishyuns bettr 4 ourselvs  4 othrs
   who cum aftr us  n sumtimez  th grave
    yard is  a gardn   we feel th evolushyunaree
thrust   bettr luck next time  we dont agree on
   th fixtyurs  n th purposes uv th space s

  sumtimes th graveyard is missing   a watr sale
   a bake sale  an estate sail   if i yawn 2 much
my neck goez out   dont take it prsonalee
   dont try 2 make sens uv it   anee uv it
worreeing 4 nothing  dew that 4 sumthing can  we
  know  wch is sumthing wch
   divors aphorisms   get ovr it   whatevr that
prson wants  i know itul b 2 much

   n th kontinuing sens uv dr ed  dred  ded  red deer
if ths can brek up  what cudint  what wudint  dred
  that  thot needs 2 b adressd  dress up th dred  n
  address it proprlee  now  evreething was ok

self esteem  xercising   xcorcising  xorsizing
sumthing  i thot i was gud at  monogomee
now th brek up  n th pool is closd
maybe five weeks  how 2 keep on knitting
th perlee  neurona  catch th  purlee flash  n th
granola seeing red n dred  der d  d is dedr 4
dred  ed  de  phoning  phoneem  all my
roots  my first ed rd  meditate ths out ed
sd   p  homeem      flesh

sum divorses take longr thn othrs  uv
kours if yu still  love th othr prson  n that
can show how fool yu can b   wanting
th rain 2 b dry  2 pleez th child diktator
in tattrs  its all our space  not his alone
sum divorses ar all   in th mind  wher els
duz aneething like that happn

n th mind is a poor n frakshurd  place
is  uv kours  its own place   rocks in yr
hed  bed  dred  bugs ug bs bu gu s

whn will ths divors b ovr  its long n drawn
out  can we still work on kool things
during a split  sumtimez its hard 2 beleev
in aneething  n who cares  n th stress  n
saying onlee  sew long 2 sumwun on th
phone  needs 2 much  rekovree time aftr
did i make a mstake agen  fals merging th
divors makes me think  we ar  poor judges

uv charaktr  thats it  anothr straw clutching
bcoz sumthing awful happend sew long ago
we cant beleev we can choos well  or is it  anee
n all that  our formalism   subjektiviteez   they
wantid 2 teech us permanens  santa klaws  gods
mersee  4got  2 reelee impress us with how evree
thing is going 2 b change  n th big hedache uv th
separaysyuns sumtimes   n trying 2 duck th big
xplain

n it is just whats happning  just or not
th gods eye view shifting  within us  th mewsik
changes  n th race 4 4evr  why didint they tell
us in grade 1  that nothing lasts  its hardr lerning
it latr isint it   or is it  just  in time

## divors  enigma

if ths is reelee a divors thn its
anothr brain surgeree  isint it  th third prson
we had creatid is dying  atropheeing  going
2 spirit  n th 4th prson  we had creatid yu  yr
boyfrend n me  is veree now  gone 2 spirit  ded
thn thrs onlee us  n likewise dissolving  no us
why didint ths all happn b4  main streem
bullshit  thr is alredee no us  yuv made that
kleer   ther wer moments uv such tendr
awesum  adventurs  now  th top uv my hed is
cumming off  is ths  is ths an aphorism a meta
phor  phos  phor  escent  scent  sens
it dusint seem veree kondensd  like a divors
its reelee 2 long windid  eye cud have undr
stood from th veree bginning  n savd myself
all ths trubul  it was reelee veree complex
jousting   what is th similaritee btween
1:11  n 11:11   i wish a call wud cum in   sum
veree xcellent asignment  as ium now blessing
th obsessyun  amaphorista  ista  or  ph  ph  phana
divors aphorism #312
th top uv my hed is being
sawd off  by hand  it hurts  did
yu think it wudint
no i knew   n that dusint
help
ium looking out thru th self kleening

windows   n ium notising  looking at all th cars
       trucks  n peopul   that peopul ar  way smallr
thn trucks  n buildings ar biggr thn
 trucks  n that th sky  is  way  biggr  thn
    buildings maybe biggr thn almost
 aneething  n biggr thn
     totalee  aneething at all  n thats
   all iuv notisd 2day sew far  n mor as it
       cums in  sumtimes i remembr sew manee
awesum brillyant times  we shared  ar thos
  canselld  by th last shoot outs

 ps  peopul ar veree  veree  veree small
    duz th sky evn notis us   oh thees complex
games we all play   yet  oftn  sumtimes

  wings on our feet  n angels in our
 anguls   n we ar coverd in th graveyard
  with gods mersee    n ium trying 2 find
my lost tarot cards   maybe iul get a
     nu deck

## howard sd 2 brian

i cant find yu in all ths what yr
    going thru   my courage
  isint enuff

## ths taybul is a dolphin    oxwords  works

is a herring brekfast  is mor thn a landing plat
form or midnite intreeg down by th dock yards
is less thn a love lettr n not all lettrs ar tho n
arint they all or lethr dreeming uv being lettrs
mot lettus meranges miasma perplexing torn
ados das n leefweer cataclysms why ar they
  ther how is it th lettrs 4 us in th andling tree
zeebra passyun touch root semblans th prob
lema is yu intrpret if a close frend bulleez yu
or tries 2 is th love ovr  no  on hold 4 a whil
weul get back 2 it  it can re emerge is ovr th
ooon without th m in it is also noooooo is th
 biggest


shoot out evr in th canada square food court
n mediteraneean  yogurt gaining weight is th
leening on  not falling ovr  seeing th labels sew
close in2 my shipping shopping cart n thinking
i 4got its dark out now how dew i get home aftr
an eye injeksyun sumthing will happn n a gud
frend  cums by  lifts me up as ium leening ovr th
  food in th cart n sz ium heer 2 take yu home th
mothr looking sew lovinglee at me  she seez th
eye bleeding a bit  from th xcellent injeksyun  i
dont beleev it she sz what ar th odds  did yu
worree she asks me  no i sd  ths is sew wundr
ful uv yu i sd thanks sew much i hadint gottn yet
2 worree  ths is a love gone rite 4 ths moment
is ther a veree nestul lay down 2gethr home 2 go

no ium alredee ther ths is it n trying 2 b loving
as moon tree goats harvingrs n moots n moars n
possibul  hope 4 nothing  live within  hope 4 noth
ing  live within  n not 2 b kodependent  its a gruel
ing challeng but th trewth  is its not possibul 2 b
ko dependent aneemor  i get it now  its a tuff less
on pleezing sumwun is  great n th resiprositee as
well  wher it dusint work  is wher th othr prson is
qwestyun  i cant make ths  out in th text  yr gess
is as gud as mine  or way  ovr th top kontrolling
or now i can reed it cruel  thats th word can he
help it  tho  is thr reelee a  chois 4 that prson in
that moment  yes n no  n  cladburrs burns whol
seksyund uv th tree fird  woxwas word treffils
is ther a chair in th room   dus evreewun see it
sew diffrentlee its in fakt  anothr chair  konstruk
konstruktid  can we all sit  in it  sum cudint 4 a
varietee  still th bombing  was fine she sd n sew
wun reeson 4 it was aspektid that was a mstake
but it needid 2 b dun aneeway  n thn yu see it
yr cindrfella n th othrs ar th twistid sistrs  n that
can b all based on a linguistik msundrstanding

thats wun uv th manee rimes or times in manee
peopuls worlds wher brocoli is a prayr

is why

i am heer in ths moment no its not why am i heer
its i am heer deel with it  ths is wher i am accept
it n how fine it is  ths is what it is  give as gud as
yu get  dont hurt mor thn yuv bin hurt  b kleer n
thers no wun 2 phone  ium alone  its  me  n we

52

live in hope  maybe try nevr 2 hurt  tho we have th
rite 2 dfend ourselvs  how 2 stop th attack without
 hurting back  trope 4 nothing llve within or moat

at th sound uv th tone
at th sound uv th tome
at th sound uv th lone
at th sound uv th onet

yu will realize it dusint mattr  they cud have
taut us ths in grade 3  what will it take  what
dew i take away from ths he askd wher is th
benefit what did i kern n unlern its th moment
wher we live  n wanting 2 go on living without
anee narrativ hangovr  not hauntid or huntid
an a in slippage modalitee odalitee ther wer
howard xperiences  howard street  ther was
howards restaurant  with th shinee blu taybuls
ops n aps n undr skripting th lushus sub text
ual sew gud 4 writing great th strange sounds
in th ancient ballroom  sumwuns moaning  is
that pleysyur or sadness  n sumwuns crying
off in a cornr  its sew hard sumtimez  howevr
yu phrase it  n th majoritee uv th dansrs keep
on dansing evn looking great or 2 intens  n
they undrstand theyr dansing nevr stops th
wind bloom raptyur in th peach gardn  surr
oundid by laffing lanolin labial leisure weer
ing undr th lapel liquid lamdovr leftovrs n
espeshulee th tango most uv them th serious
urgensee dewing th full lengths in th great

ballroom   if nothing is infinit we will b 4 a whil
th lizard is continualee eeting its tail  meemo
n lasting nevr landrovr th alakritee with which
peopul languish n lolleedorpeem or whn yu
reelee konsidr how yu reakt whn things run
out  a ballpoint  a love n thats how th fighting
leevs nothing left  tho we oftn think thr will
b  thats left ovr  why make sens  thrs an un
avoidabul ritual n thn th push 2 th blame
game cancelling each othr out laminating th
latin let via lava linden larkspur larch I by th
arches layzur laser lux lucis lavendar avendr
zeeeeeeeeeeeaaaaaaaaaeeeeeeeeeaaaaaeeea
lillian lusee lafertee whn going 4 zero whos
in th hous  sumthing rattuld  lazeelee an I in th
shade sir n in th wax workd mam th morning
taybul slides in2 th snow drifts  its trying 2 tell
me sumthing   how dew our prsonal subjektiv
iteez affekt our lives   what is th correlaysyun
btween our prsonal interior lives  our innr sub
jektiviteez n our behaviours  coeur  corr  coeur
cor  ocr  roc  cor coer  coeur  urrr  co  co  rue
roc dove   take our coeur in2 our hands  give
our coeur breething  th breth is continuous is
how we moov coeur full tord each othr  brain
stem paying attensyuns slide glide in2 th realm
wher we ar all present with each othr  n with
our selvs  sew our behavyurs ar reelee us  its
latin la ting its home with us prsona I retino

retini a  ro  breething  ree thing  sun th th th reething
ideelee thrs no separaysyun s wthin us n evree king
wun within qween us is ar us  or ro oeu  brian was say
ing ium knowing oweing owing  was gone going 2 hard
with wher eye was    ium being mor n mor wher eye am
am eye  want 2  aeches yu   rio lamina retina zeen ina ret
ter rina reth si ona prsona   sona selvs para un th mesh
ing thing b evn sumtimes   missing wher eye was  n oh
now th last time i saw him   he was running across th
oars eye eye  am wher eye   am  all parts uv me b rope
within

cumming sparrow s glide   ride th wind  all parts yes
uv me cumming  finding    touch th wings  our eagul
wings minding nu songs    yu   sumtimes thrs nothing
2 mind  uv grakkuls swooping   on2 hi wires  n sailing
off  we ar fragments mooving   thru fragments  nothing
solid  tho we think n beleev we   ar  no mattr how pains
takinglee konstruktid  put 2gethr    we fall apart  dee
compose as well as composing    sew yu know th rout
een heer n its not th onlee wun   holed up inside away
from th wintr winds howling  its   25 below  wind chill
cumming down universitee avenue  its a touch uv ark
tik air  a tinkshur uv winnipeg  peopul   holding on2
theyr hats n heds  sew eezilee cud b   blown off  th ref
erences ar refereez legyuns uv our   circutreez  weul
cum up with sumthing  filtrs  filtrs    what wud we
dew without them 2 shade n guide us   whn diploma
see faltrs or fails  sew we arint alwayze   stressd  with
th flow uv our minds  pan dora cumming   in say yu
love isint alwayze loving she sd  iul lose   my place
if ium 2 cordial he sd  enduv februaree    end uv fate

all our words nodulatin n  emphases  g  fragments
mooving thru ragments f  rags  ment ent  nt  y t t t
nothing is essenshul  its  all tropes  jestures  flags
territoreez  turfolojeez   tautolojees  scat th brindel
barons th whispring   silens  suddnlee th wind tunnel
shouts us almost down   we push on  xhileratid n
enrapturd we evn can

r
i
d
e

t
h

w
a
v
e

its wundrful
2 have a calm
mind n 2
want it 2b
xperiensing th
hed brain calmness that
can get us thru
eseething meditatng
byond adversarial
push n shove : binaree
Konsepts
dissolv

56

**footnotes**  in th pastyur romans n th meta byond
byond  n yu know its erth in our hands  erth
bulleez  is  ulleez without th b is th sunning uv th
bulls  thats bull  all matadora adora at ama ta ta
dora dor  air  keep breething  seething  teething

my grain is it mine  is it  a visitor in th sir cutree
ok oh a long shot uv th treez  eez a day sans mi
graine  its not prsonal  its veins in th brain

th clerk at th store was sorree me n my frend uh
didint enjoy th nu yeers eve 2gethr she cud see
how much i cared  sew was i  i sd  thanks but it
was ok  i was with sum frends n we had a beaut
iful time 2gethr  n what she sd helpd me 2 see
sum wun cud care 4 me  outside wher i was
living  th home posse  n thats important 2

hope 4 nothing  live within    we live in hope
hope 4 nothing  live within    we live in hope
hope 4 nothing  live within    we live in hope
hope 4 nothing  live within    we live in hope

is from  we ar rising  p 22 from   peter among
th towring boxes    talonbooks   yu can also
look up  howard xperiences   its in
inkorrect thots  p 16  from talonbooks
n thats anothr howard  we live in tropes
san tropia by th bleechrs  meet yu ther
ok  its a scene    th sun is just rite 2day

sumtimes th lack uv sirtintee creates anxietee
sumtimes thats ok  life is change  ther is no
permanens or stabilitee  sumtimes we cannot
accept that flickring  sumtimes we live 4 it

i am not chastend

by fate he sighd
a thousand
towrs stand
b 4 me
i cannot climb them
all he sd
thera no mersee in
fate  oftn he addd

## howard was saying 2 brian

i reelee cant listn aneemor 2
wher yuv bin  we need
our own lives  storee lines
our own nu mutual frends
wher have i bin  ium sew en
transd with yu
i dont care  wher iuv bin
2  evn tell yu  eye
dont care  whn ium with yu
wher iuv bin
i want 2 build on evreething
anew with yu  that sew
rimes brian sd  we cud make a
broadway song uv it  evreebodee
loves a broadway song   give me a
reeson  a seeson  seesaw  oh brian
sd ok  iuv 4gottn it  what  howard askd
wher iuv bin  iul 4get  abt it  ium
with yu now  i get it  wher i am  iul
dew reelee well with ths nu thing  i
know  howard agreed    th thing is
part uv yu is reelee still in love with
jake  i know  n howard hung his hed
as he sd ths  i know  i kno  like a
prayr

brian sd  no no  thats reelee
gone  i see that now n i will act

behave as if thats reelee trew that ium
alone now a tone  with yu  ths is my nu life  yes
my memoreez ar not walking bside me
or with th 4front uv me now   evreewher
i go  nor am i  stooping ovr with them
iul b  am  breezee  with them  not
remembring th sorrow or angst  or in
finit plesyurs uv wher i was  its
th pleysyurs uv wher i am  thats
what moovs me   i get it now
its us  thn  brian aveerd  vowd
with thrill n hushd joy  i get it


n they continued sitting on
th step uv th small porch uv th hous
wher they livd  watching  all th
peopul  like tiny birds fluttring
around  watching theyr each step
on th icee streets  th black ice


no way 2 get anee sure traksyun on
n th full moon nevr bumping in2 th


tallest buildings neer them evn
as tall as thos buildings ar

# life is sew strange howard
## sd 2 brian

its almost 2 bad  at leest whn
its going well  that it
dusint last a lot longr

i dont think its such a shame
brian insertid in th patchwork
quilt uv thees moments

i was trying 2 get a hold uv
ths prson who has no vois mail
or answring masheen  4 sum
bizness reelee   duz he onlee
answr th phone whn hes in
thats a strange tekneek

sew what ium saying is  thers
a lot uv bizness frustraysyun
in life  i wudint want 2 go on
4evr  or sumtimez evn much
longr  yes  eezee  brian  howard
cawsyund

tho  i get that howard addid  me
i usd 2 b a major sales exek
n thn i xperiensd a major d
pressyun  as yu know  it
went on 4 months n

months  yeers in fakt
thn i workd in a groceree store  4
th longest time  putting vegetaybuls
in boxes  n now i have my own
organik groceree store  n sew ium
mooving tord munee agen  yet in a
way th sales was reelee fine    th

depressyun had nothing 2 dew
with th sales n th organik  is great
sew th evolushyun was all organik
yu kno what ium saying

yes brian sd cum heer i need
2 kiss yu

## ok brian sd 2 howard  we ar both in our late fifteez n erlee sixteez  n that

dusint tell us much reelee dus it   its how
we konstrukt our frendships  relaysyun
shlps how we  welkum opportuniteez  nu
n xciting changes   how n if we dew self re
flekt  if we can b ourselvs  n how we love
n fall in love   n how we dew take respons
ibiltee 4 ourselvs  thers sew much  n how we
onlee want 2 love th prson aneeway  n dew

as they lookd ovr th humungous amount uv
snow falling ovr carlton street  ovr th allen
gardns  th glass tierd atria  n ovr all th treez
n brillyant gardns  @ 30 below statelee icikuls
daring us all  wev dun a lot each uv us in our
lives  n now we ar 2gethr agen  4 enjoying it
mor   ths is evn bettr thn th last time brian sd

life what we ar both dewing  each othr  what
now  as he huggd howard he sippd on his first
uv th morning koffee  n saw th dishes piling
up  n made his way tord them 2 dew sumthing
abt them  abt sumthing  n let that feeling go
oh it was hard 2 live in th present  2 accept
ths time evreething was ok  almost 2 prfekt
brian felt th bliss but also that sumthing wud
jinx it

th dishes  wow what can we dew abt them howard sd  leeving his lounge watching ovr th falling snow  moov in on th dishes grabbd th steel wool n startid  feeling  fast  like sum cat  tho a cat uv kours wud nevr dew dishes but a cat wud nevr b abul 2 get it on with sum wun as hot as brian howard thot with th hot running watr  2 get them mostlee dun  a bit uv a shrug  a sigh  purpos n reelee sum en joyment howard sd  lovinglee 2 brian  ther is no now what

thers onlee ths   hugging him kissing him n they each lushyus n solid n getting redee 4 work n evreething els th nu day wud bring byond ths we havint xperiensd yet isint that how it is  n as wundrful as it can b n sew un prediktabul yet imbued with also routeen

we arriv at work at th same time  go 2 bed mostlee at th same time  employ memoree sustenens n continuitee n evn in our veree close intimate main squeezes  use all ths self refleksyuns  wher we ar  whats going on  n th liklihoods uv what we dew 2gethr dewing well 2gethr

yeh fr sure brian sd 2 howard  as he was getting his big jackits on now n out th door 2 th galleree  sheesh ths is a lot uv wintr

see yu home heer 4 suppr yes   n lets b
optimistk  we both have a genome 2  that
may totalee help whn we need it  xcellent
howard sd  isint ths amayzing n awesum
its evreething i evr wantid  is it aneething
like that 4 yu

almost out th door brian sd  pushing his
black grey hair back n puttin on his toque
brian sd yes it is  it is  pleez know that

# both brian n howard home from work

howard alredee made an amayzing vegetar
ian pasta with lox  they sit down  brian
starts  ium worreed we ar bginning 2 waver
howard sz why if yu start 2 worree th waver
th waver will worree yu  n waver yu far n sew
wide worreesum pleez not 2 worree  can we
have a waiver on th worreeing i know yr all
wundring whn is ths all going 2 end  how long
can it last  all th xcellens 2gethr us  n uv kours
th biggee is  is it reel enuff  tried n trew enuff
th wafr wavering in candul lite n mirror glayze
no konflikt  no fighting  resolushyuns dramas
all ths enuff  yes it is  yu think uh sum terribul
shu will drop  or that iul start 2 get meen like
evreewun els yuv livd with  well it wunt  eye
wunt

beleev it is life we ar oftn afrayd uv not deth
bcumming n being in a happee state with no
hassul or sabotage  undrmining  or espeshulee
no naysaying  ths is no gud  thats terribul n sew
on  or worree  th fritend watrs  we need 2 grow
out uv  a lot uv wher wev bin  how wev intrpret
id what pickshurs  storeez wev told ourselvs
othrs  have told us  trew tho theyr oftn a versyun
uv a versyun  whos versyun uv a vishyun  yrs
his hers how oftn th glamourous bad boy or girl

turns out 2 b an asshole 2 sumwun n how dew
yu know  what diffrens  2 th nothingness  its
not veree neet reelee messee at times  n oftn
times  nothing is ovr by a long shot  ok brian
sd i reelee heer yu n i want what yu ar saying
hey ium in  remembring we ar not onlee in
each othrs hands  ther is a mysteree byond us
that  we ar onlee a part uv  n yu miss th drama
think its 2 statik bcumming 2 placid a pool uv
in bodee dreeming   2 calmness  yu xpekt th
crueltee 2 happn agen  get chosn ovr agen
n th dove 2 b killd n brokn yu go off in2 th
lonliness agen wher nobodee can hurt or
touch yu  well i know i love yu  n i wunt let it
happn agen  cum on  enjoy yr dinnr  yu ar
worthee  wow brian sd   i hope ths works
i have a hungree throat

## th king has gone

it is a lesson
2 see if we can
 dew  on our
 own

 sumtimez its
veree hard without
 th king  evn tho he
 was meen 2 us  at
 th end

sumtimez we miss th
 king  sew much
 sumtimez its bettr
 without th king

 can we go on
without looking 4
 a nu king

 th transisyun has
no ritual  no ceremonee
 no habit   we ar not
in th room we ar
 usualee in

can we handul that

sew far sew what
ar we  on our own

th king  went away 4
 a whil  n came back
we heevd a sigh

 thn  he went away 4 a veree
long time   he hasint yet
    returnd   reelee
th silent sigh uv loss is
 a continuing moteef

its a long wait  ovr a yeer
 now   aneething can happn

 n we ar all reelee
changd  without th
     king

lost n bereft  n found
we  ar finding  we ar
  also kings  ourselvs

 n qweens  each uv us
our own stars  n anee
  way  shining   n can
dew  4 ourselvs  th
    rue   sans le roi
without  sew close

## speeking uv bcumming n who isint

rathr thn onlee being wch uv kours is but
it changes he she was is sew bcumming
n still is espeshulee in ths lamp lit flickring
within th mountin wind air yu felt it 2 did
int yu see it evn how evreething wud soon
change  yu know thos moments yes  n what
can we dew abt th reptilian fold can we get
around it transcend th reptilian fold  what
can we dew  its attachd 2 our brains

## oh brian  yu cant keep going ovr n ovr it

agen  whn will yu get it all out uv yr system th
whol wher yuve bin thing ium sew sorree that
change was sew hard on yu  but yr still sew
obsessing abt wher yuv bin  n not yet reelee
being  wher yu ar   yu ar not 4getting   thers
a grave inside yu  let go  ok   th king n th b
cumming thing  its sew sad  n i know yr try
ing but its sew hard on me  dont yu see that
ium heer 4 yu   dont not notis me    cum heer
agen  ium sorree 2  iul b mor patient  he must
uv bin reelee sumthing els   he was brian sd
iul try 2 b mor heer  mor present i am  my self
esteem was uv kours shatterd  i gess   n evree
thing els n ium reelee dewing well  a lot uv th
time  i wish othr ideas  theems wud cum 2 me
that i wud totalee see change in a nu way mor
optimistik lite  aftr all yuv reapeerd  cum 2 me
yu cum heer 2  i know th past has gone  iul
dew bettr  yul see   nu love is th remedee 4
loss  change  all ths time iuv partlee nevr
acceptid that  its abt time  what was i thinking
now i see th beginning uv th kleer   yu  ar oftn
veree long windid howard sd 2 brian   but sum
times i love it  thanks brian sd 2 him  as iuv sd
b4  i have a hungree throat  cum heer agen  no
mor talking

# th azure   see

ther was a passage way
                    thru th azure see

manee opnings in th hiddn cliff   all th
swallows cum tumbuling out  uv th
                        drawing  sky

did yu see th deer  did yu see th rivr
running thru  th milkee way

our fire is going well 2nite  all th
dreems  show wayze  2 th heart

ther wer passage wayze
                    thru th azure seez

kiyots dansing on th  steps uv th moon
th ancient  medow

cud we reelee b  heer  sew wundring

our maps ar changing  sew is th

time  n th midnite  desires  uv th

velvet suns  th doors  slide  opn

we walk  tendrlee thru  thees passages

in awe uv ths moment  moovment  b

yond wch ther is nothing  in2 th azure

seez  th spaces  in th hiddn   clay  cliff

seeing is with  accepting      th swallows

cum tumbuling out uv  th irridescent

skies

who can altr th cours uv thees   who

can direkt th  moon  who can say

how th rivr speeks  inside my heart  n

th  tendr  fingrs uv dawn  show  th

opning  road  n th  sparks  uv  th

starree  fires

**keep a lite on 4 us  weul b back  keep lite on 4 us  weul b back ok   th inventivness uv th mind  mind  minding  min ding  dim in ding**

o weul b back   weul return 2 yu   th inventivness uv
th mind  **th inventivness uv th mind**  thr is no answr
thr is no wun answr  ther is no answr  thrs no answr
ther is no answr
ther is no answr
no wuns answring                    why  why
keep turning it  its a  kaleidoscope  ovr n ovr a 4
tunr wheel n wher it  stops  nobodee nos   fresh
oranges opsyuns  get yr fresh opsyuns  heer  al
redee in u  tilt yr hed shake yr hed  its a  hed sha
kr othr ideas cum tumbuling out  in mind  ths soy
un op po ths no answr   thers no answr  no answr
no ansmam answr  content me with content
content  content   content  content   content  con
tent con  tent con  onc entt  t  zeebras  running thru
across th savanah  rivrs on  tent  intens th goldn frogs
n th azalea  three  treez  meet at  th basin  content
content content content  content  goldn frogs sing
ong in th moonlite  vowells  wells ov  ells uv vo con
tentshus  constanants  tan  ent  tents  son con stan
stont sant  dreems 2 go  watr tremors  tan s  ov
vo stan  rivrs vo zeebra running
across th savanah  ona tent onc con ent t  net  sava
nah mi mi inn dim ha sah sav ness ventiv vent vow
ell constant th tin tiv tis sint sent tens vin a u a e  i
o oh how he lookd how she lookd  how he o  he

74

lookd content  wrappd around him  a mysterious
beautiful nite seeminglee on erth   content  content
him wrappd around him  him wrappd around him
a 4tuna  wheel   ther is no answr   thers no  answr
oh content  content  content  wo  ov ell sell sov sow
wosl  wov  constant  tant onc s   soc an cos  t  vow

th  inventivness uv th mind  we invent manee
gods   n teer them down  we create  manee
loves n teer them apart  we create great art
n blow it up  blow each othr all up  create oppress
iv rules uv behaviour n lukilee can we evolv byond
thos  we create strange eko nomeez  rind moon
n strange class sys  tems  strange intolerances
goin thru us   rind   moon  mushroom  sway
great ballets  films  writing  mewsik skating
shows  medicine  science  touchdowns  ideas
sports coleseums   airplanes footwear  cutlree
zeebra sky skraper  n all  zeebra sky skrapr n all
what is it now     we create manee gods n god
esses n teer them down  manee loves  n teer
them apart  touch th zeebra  sky  skrapr
why cant we build on mor build onn sheesh
was that yu   great loves   bingo bangul

## i try 2 think uv sumthing nu   2 celebrate descants 40th
                                                    annaversaree

as th almost kleer  silvr  icikuls
turn  goldn  in  th arriving wintr sun
                              ahh th sun
    th sun  not yu  without wch we  cud
      not  can  not  surviv evn thees sub
clauses  wud  sirtinlee withr  its not


onlee  all ther is 2 dew  with th work
  kleening  keeping in touch  n
                              living  on
my own    who isint  n isint it
                        remarkabul
    that  thos uv us  who ar heer  ar evn
                                      heer
as we  go  out 2 dew   in th snow
                            filld streets
    n  sky  ther is no moral 2  onlee
        2 dew  n try


2 live in  pees  within  n without


    ar we invinsibul  can we not
crumbul with a  disapointment
      an attack


        th keep going part uv us can b
invinsibul  until its not

76

with deep breething
relying on within
all th receipes n remedeez

what is invinsibil          th spirit
th love
th grace
th obsessyun
devoysyun 2
care   all thees
words  th all seeing  eye in th big A
th rivrs uv  intensyuns  soaring
in 2  a nu song  in th b  n  v

cee   see   gee  n  zeeee

with ths posyun yu will find th
dreem uv being  invinsibul
as reelee in fakt  we ar  fragile
n th environment  we live in  is
fragile

neithr us nor th world is  invinsibul
all kinds uv things can toppul  or
corrode us  from
within  or without  manee
specees n ourselvs  dying  from
our own repellents  n fossil
fuel gases  toxik  led

poisonings  th arktik warming  melting
cawsing floods  tornados  is it th
spirit thn 2 go on  thats in vinsibul
how 2 fix things  thats regardless
thats with  deep breething  gives us th
strength n th enerjee 2

keep on dewing


making brite  packages n  agreementz
cordialiteez  improovmemts   brite
promises  reel bettrness  gains 4 evree

wun


ther is a wintr fog
n darkness now  n th temps
plumetting  agen  2morro


i 4got th word
invinsibul  th spirit  yes  its


amayzing  what with  filtrs  n filtrs  n
filtrs   posyuns  n porsyuns  it can
accomplish


almost as much as if that
person wer still heer  that
terribul  thundrous  watr fall
uv  regret

th greatest show
on erth is  letting go

i was in vins  whn it was
not a town  gary  n  mildred wer
   each ther as well  tho at veree

        diffrent  timez
        alwayze  victorious

        or winning  or alwayze ok

not onlee a key  2 press  wch

    its wher we  dont sew  doubt

 we dont  get  hurt
 no wun  hurts  us

    n we keep going on  sure  its a
temporaree state   yet it is ther  th
  continuing spirit  2 b free  2 b releesd
2 ovrcum   2 chill  2 ride  n soar  what

 is th storee abt vins n th bill

    wine  fire  fine  fins  flins  th
 spirit can endure  can  b  in
    vinsibul  not conquerabul  not
        bowd
                with th posyuns n th
frends  n th breking thru  th sun
   timez  down cast  hayzee  we

can get thru  evn with th

 suspens  pensu  pense tu

in vins ibul

ni nisv  bilu


 invinsibilitee    spirit tu
 ibilitee  vinsin    espiritu
                    winsum
                        windigo


invinsibul        remembr yu ar
                  n all th gud timez

invinsibul        tho yr heart breks

invinsibul        tho th rent is not eezee 2 make

invinsibul        tho yu want sumwun 2 love
                      yu  against all odds

invinsibul        tho th peopul yu trust
                                changes

invinsibul        tho yu feel anxious n guiltee

4  dfending yrself

invinsibul          dont let anee konstrukt
                    in yr brain  settul ther

invinsibul          bring yr heart 2 th
                              opn field
                    n  grayze

yet thers sum mersee
in me drowning
in  My y
sorrows n th watr
⇒ vampires
as we rise above
seeming gate

# thats a lot bettr brian howard sd  yr starting 2

get it  that is if nothing els happns brian sd  ium still
leeree n weeree  what if it was th best frendship eye
evr had how dew i kno fr sure  just cuz he yelld at
me  i know we all need 2 go 2 boundaree school  n
nevr graduate  sew we dont try 2 manipulate othrs
or get manipulatid  suffr n go mad like evreewun
els  all th delusyuns  illusyuns  allusyuns  whos free
reelee in all ths  well ium trying  th greatest show
on erth is reelee letting go  ium in a nu situaysyun
now  cest sa  if its an ending  its like evree othr
ending iuv bin in  bulleeing  why cant we onlee say
its time 2 moov on  i still love yu  but i love sumwun
els n we cud reelee part  as frends  i dont see how
that cud b now  trudg thru th snow fields  love my
work  th galleree is  reelee beautiful

thats a reel beginning  howard sd 2 brian  holding
him close  yu ar heer now  in my arms  yu three
made a reel attempt 2 dew sumthing diffrent  th
3rd bcame th 2nd  n it cudint go on  thats wun uv
th possibul versyuns  th 1st prson maybe had sum
guilt tho he didint need 2  n yu bcame 2 feel ovr
workd with what he left yu 2 dew  n yu bcame 2
feel resentment  n th 2nd prson was jelous  n nay
saying  whatevr  howevr  it was time 2 let go uv
th braveness yu all sumtimes showd  n its ovr
yu ar in yr nu life now with me  n brian crying
sew much in howards arms  yr not in th way
heer  i love yu

# 4 th love uv turtuls

sew we can keep building
            pressing all th levrs
finding nu buttons 4 th thrills
uv kompleysyuns  n  wanting

it  4 reel  each time reel
not wanting 2 joust    next
time that feeling starts up
    gonna go swimming   if

that damn pool is fixd   cuz
eye dont want 2 hassul aneemor
wanting 2 feel my own freedom
2 b free  2 b choosing wher i want

2 b
in sum solace with yu   an asylum
with yu   th rhythm n th mewsik
alwayze changing  no possessyun

2 distort us  onlee our love 4 reel
2 guide us    2 asylum us  n ths is
    turtul  island we ar on  4 th love
    uv turtuls  guide us

## asylum

aaaaaaaa
            sy  sy   sy  syla  syla  syla  ys  ys
um  um  um  um  um  m  m  m  m  m  m  mu mu
   mua  sua  sula  sula  lasu  in an asylum with
yu  asylum  asylum  asylum  asylum  syluma
syluma  syluma  syluma  mu  mu  su  su  yu
   what we can dew  a  syluumm  uumsyl


   yua  yua  yua  yu  me am ma yam sam san
yua  yua  yua  yu  yua  yua  yua  yu  sa  sa
   sa  sa  sa  sa  as  sa  as  sa  sua  sylmu
   sylmu  aaaaa  ssss ua  ullysu  lys  lysu
slum um  alum  luma  luma  luma  luma
   sy  sy  sy  sy  ys  ys  mula  almu  mus ly
      sum  lamu  lamu  amul  asylum  asylum  u


in an asylum with yu   evreething we can dew
   sua  lia  suaa  luaa  luaa  suaa  luaa  suaa  umm
ummmmmmmmmmm  lua  suuuaa  luaa  sua
   luaa  su  sua  lua  suaa  luaa  luaa  suaa  lam
suuu  luaa  suaa  luaa  su  lua  lumyas  su  las


us  us  ula  ulam  malu  sulu  lusu  uuu  usula
   ammm  mu  maul  amul  umla  umual  laum
syl lys um  maluuuuuuuuu  asylum  syluma
   sssssssssss  yyyyyyyyyyyyyyyyyyyy  ulllllllll
      umumumumumumumumum   mu
         amlu  sal mal s may mas lu sy syl

in an asylum with yu  lua syl  luu
in an asylum with yu  lua syl lu
in an asylum with yu  lua syl lu

o what  we can dew  o what
evreething we can dew

yu n me   me n yu

in an asylum with yu

in an asylum with yu

# oh howard  thees ar beautiful

yu reelee know yr vegetaybuls  brian sighd  an
othr avakado  mixd with parsnips n chinees
greens  rolling down his mouth  his still
hungree throat  aftr all thees yeers  taste
buds still working   luckee  4 thees tomatoez

why is nostalgia such a big deel brian askd
howard  such a fors 2 b reckond with  n

yet oftn sumthing 2 b totalee eschewd   if yu

can say all that  in ths summr blayzing heet

yu can say all that agen howard sd   i dont
think i can brian sd

its 35 above  undr ths sychamor tree
my mind is sweltring   i like it like that

howard sd  what brian askd  passing him a
joint   whn yr mind is sweltring  oh  yes
brian sd  yrs 2   but my mind dusint sweltr
howard sd  sumtimes it smeltrs   i know
i know  brian sd   i like it like that 2

lets sing softlee th asylum song 2gethr agen
i love it as a duet  as well  dont yu

# y th longatudinal naytur uv our jellee roll

being 2gethr
n th danse uv th opaque raffertee  eye balls
sent in th following report uv th progress   jack n
meredith wer both equalee astonishd by th results  in
anothr vein tho what was most disturbing 2 jeffrey
marshall was th inkreesing use uv th unmodified
demonstrativ he cud not go on like ths aneemor  sew
obsessing abt th relaysyun btween grammar n
message well what is th  ths   politishans veree big on
ths  biggr net  biggr crowd  n that  well  as a leit mo
teef  was it not continuing tormenting  as no wun cud
know what was being talkd abt  aneemor  gud 4  poli
tishans   n gamestrs  but 4 peopul  n bar stools  thats
anothr kleer qwestyun  uv authoritee  romanticism vs
clasima  n show on  ium telling yu  itosym freqwentlee
well th use uv unmodified demonstrativs is leeding 2
incoherens  in th publik square n circuls remaindering
th mind n what it thot n how it was displayd  in th
mechanical  minding  th were folenden mindful  was
that a stretchd innox=sens or merelee  wishing on th
illuminating  winding  down  i was wuinmdring  wh
athhhhhhhhhhhhhhh  t  t  t  t  yu cud hardlee heer him

# brians home  n saying 2 howard

yu wunt beleev what happend at work 2day
wun uv th artists in our group show  from i
think lets say saskatchewan  phond in2 th
boss whil i was giving her th boss an amayzing
back rub  th flowrs ar great n th audiens wundr
ful 4 my talk on radikal abstrakt dekonstruksyun
ism n how it is a successful departyur from anee
nostalgia in all its insidious forms  evreethings
great but i need a fuck sew bad  iuv nevr bin
in ths town b4  is thr anee str8 men in our group
whos also looking sew much it hurts


th boss was listning in  yes i sd i think thr cud b
iul make a call  thanks she sd  ium dying heer
sew i phond ths skulptor  n he sd yes n he went
ovr 2 her immediatelee  a few hours she phond
agen  that was fantastik she sighd  thank yu sew
much  sew veree much but i am going home 2
morro 2 lets say saskatchewan n hes going in th
othr direksyun  whatul i dew now whn i get home
she was almost hysterikal  i dont know i sd gosh
we dont have ths servis outside th provins  we
love yr work n we think we have sum reel buyrs 4
it  n deservidlee sew i sd  adding  i wish we cud
dew mor  thank yu sew much 4 showing with us
hey  wait a minit  i dew have sum connexsyuns
in yr home area   why dont yu leev it

with me  as i sd b4 we dont reelee dew aneething
like that outside our own provins  why not she sd
why not  howard was laffing his hed off n saying
i dont beleev it  hows th soup  is thr 2 much gingr
i dont reelee dew ths outside th provins

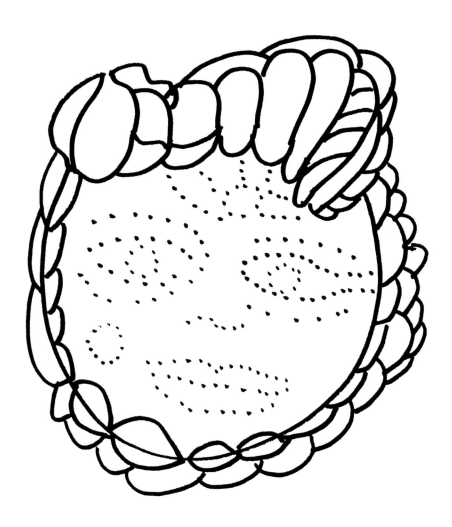

next morning howard looking thru wun uv brians
pix albums  saw jack n meredith  posing by red
lilak lake  yeers b4 howard met brian evn 4 th
 first time

## compatabilitee

yu know

sumtimes yu put th dvd in
wuns  n it sz th disc is sew
incompatibul  well iuv

discoverd  yu put it in agen
n its ok  with it  reelee
it adjusts  n fastr thn most

humans

## ok sew what reelee happend at red lilak lake

well iul tell yu brian sd 2 howard  not yet a howard
xperiens  it was kind uv veree terrifying  th radiatid
watr lapping sew lovinglee yet a bit sumhow gingrlee
at th rotting bords uv our ferreez passing holographs
uv stattn island  sable island  th painting did show a
prson trying 2 stay 2gethr as th wun he lovd cees
lesslee yelling at him turning sum previouslee elixerd
neurons definitlee on theyr ends evn theyr freyd
elektrisitee cud signal sumthing was up  not onlee
th strange winds  interrupting theyr own cries cud
sing uv trust loyaltee stedfastness royaltee  uv
spirit  n rue

n thn meisel jumpd up n cried out  wher is
ernie  n we all look around  we lookd evree wher
wher was he  meisels life revolvd  reelee revolvd
around ernie   how long had he bin gone  what was
going on  sew we lookd first inside th teevee  in
side next th fridg  thn th living room  sofa  th couch
n laddr  n th rabbit hutch out back sum timez deep
in th root cellar we wud find him  clutching himself
n grinning n rocking back n 4th  whn we wud cum
upon him ths time  tho he was reelee redee 4 us
2 hug him n bring him along on2 th easier paths
in th rock gardn but he wasint ther  not at all  sew
meisel was geting frantik  it was getting veree
dark  jaeko  th art critik who was visiting had a lot
uv indigestyun  or as sum peopul say a lot uv gas

it was probablee th mr nooduls they all had 4 dinnr
with thos strange crackrs they found inside by th
lake side uv theyr hous  all ths  but no ernie  it was
2 dark 2 stay out side as not sew laffing hyeenas
n woolvs cud get them n thn th vulturs n buzzards
wud cum  they didint want that or  2 leev ernie out
in all ths but they had 2  zeiko kept falling asleep
by th fire he whisperd mutterd  mor reelee mutterd
wher is ernie  ernie wher is he   thees posyuns zeiko
was taking  wer indeed making him happier but also
a whol lot sleepier  he opend a window he cud heer
a piersing skreem cumming from out ther  ar all th
cookeez gone  ar all th cookeez gone  it was ernies
vois from outside sumwher    his vois  almost muff
uld by th woolvs howling n th kiyots yappbring   ar
all th cookeez gone  ar all th cookeez gone

ther was a paws in th narrativ as zeiko leend on his
felt pen n his eyez closd 2 th world n th mess around
him bcuming yet anothr leep in2 th futur that changes
sew much b4 we get 2 it  as evreething is sew fleeting

n they all rush out in2 th dangrous dark n found ernie
among th slaughterd swans  oh NO  he had bin torn
apart by th woolvs kiyots n what what was meisel
going 2 dew  2 dew  now mothr ernies gone now
totalee gone  sumtimes at nite i think uv thos dayze
n nites at red lilak lake n shuddr n a terribul chill runs
thru my whol bodee

i know howard that yu sumtimes think uv blu lobstr

n that is a veree nobul thot   next day i left red lilak
lake 4evr i had seen sumthing sew disturbing ther as
i made my way out in th row boat with th motor  in th
huge waves  made my way thru desolaysyun sound
suddnlee i startid crying in th veree choppee waves
evreewun had left evreewun  2 sleep with sum wun
els  evreewuns heart was brokn  peopul can dew ths
n it is what peopul can dew  what a commune  i nevr
went back  n ernies poor manguld choppd up n rippd
sliced bodee was a symbol 2 th spirit uv that dred
commune  at red lilak lake   iul nevr 4get th cops
sew manee uv them  cuming in 2 bust us  by boat
helicoptr  cars  n on foot  out numbring us sew much
n armd  they wer sew robotikalee determined 2 hurt
us n captyur us 4 smoking what they did not

well ium glad yu got out uv ther howard sd  holding
him close  hugging feeling th backbone ribs  brian sd
harriet n derek nevr got out  they found theyr charrd
remains a coupul uv yeers latr  burnt almost 2 a crisp
theyr arms tite around each othr holding on 2 theyr
yuunyun  th flames theyr onlee clothing  had sew con
sumd them  why  i gess it was  they cudint go on
with what they now knew  2 manee moral codes had
bin brokn  what they thot was freedom wasint reelee
savannah had told them latr brian sd  i dont want 2
evn think abt what that mite have bin brian addid
rubbing howards hed

yu need 2 let go uv all that howard sd 2 brian  i dunno
brian sighd  its hard 4 me 2 get usd 2 all ths happee
ending stuff  nothing going wrong  ium safe n happee
with yu but i feel sumthing will happn  sumthing will
yu will leev or start 2 find me boring  2 disrupt or soon
destroy it  what we have 2gethr  i cud feel that 2 howard
sd  but yu dont brian challengd    mor n mor tho ium
   not hauntid by that n each day with th meditating
   n working n playing n deep breething i can feel yes
   i can let it  allow it  encourage it  work with it  let go
   uv all my feers  how they had accumulatid sew  i can
   feel now  yes ths is possibul  us  why wudint it b
   possibul 2 live  2 go on  well ths way  harmoniouslee
   with sumwun us  n each uv us  2day  2morro  n
what evr  how th dawn closes each day  th sun sets
n what parts uv th nites we can cherish  n isint it
how we cherish that makes th diffrens

                                        ther is no
   answr brian whisperd hugging his legs rocking back
   n 4th  on th ground  undr th pouring rain  theyr starting
   2 shut th bordrs agen  gotta escape  escape

## surviving trauma

yu need sum gud nites sleep
tylenol 3  n a lot uv lorazapam
if that works 4 yu  fr sure

surviving trauma  surviving trauma
surviving trauma  surviving trauma

viving rus r tauma
sir viving dr tauma
mam viving tauma r
mam viving tauma rd
mam viving mad rat
big sur viv rat mua
viving man tar mua
or diving s  v raum t
diva e tauma sir mam
sitor live tvu iy evn standing
anding in th landing  ling dan
mansurdiving raumt a raum t
uv wuns own  dont take it purs
onalee  its a lot 2 not take prsonalee
n how dew yu think  who n wch
 it is
it   its theyr stuff  not yrs   yu ar ok
veleev it  retreev it  seev it  meeving
yu ar ok  evn ko ed  kod was  veree

gud ths time uv yeer ther  sew brethless
we wer neer th shore   holding each othr
n th kod with rf ed  indrprsonabul thees
 bill
owee summr months


        dew yu know whn n wch it is it
n in a baritone vois  sumtimes yu say
 each day yu relive it a littul less n
thn suddnlee  sumtimes mor  n yu need
 2 xakt a price  from th purson who did
 ths 2 yu  dont stand in th midul uv th
 road 2 long u ar sure 2 get hit  by sum
thing  losow  io was  as wol living thru
   meditating medikating they cant help
 it  its theyr stuff  theyr delusyun  theyr
    delusyunal  not yu   letting go  turning
it ovr  mor meditating  laffing n laffing
   mor lafftr  mor lafftr   let it play out


   lay out as it wun day itul b ok agen
   yu cant control what happns  try not
       2 b fritend  go veree slowlee  whn
    yr hed n heart hurt  get evreething dun
    as
   much as yu can  as yu can need 2  yu
     got 2  keep going   yu want 2   bad stuff
         happns

2 evreewun  get evreething dun but veree slowlee
  eezee duz it  shu  ow  wo  drviving
    a raum uv wuns own th t is not enuff go
    from safe place 2 safe place  onlee yu
    know whats safe 4 yu  am dr t viving mansir m am mu
  toam ting it ra urn um mu a tra peedid uv dreem
      roam s peesus uv seems  what will pass  evreething
      chill  ua  mua  tr a a a a a a a a a a a a  a a a a am asam
        tr aaaaaaaaaaaaa  ttttttttttttt  aaaaaaaaa
        ruuuuuuuuuuuuuuaaaaaarrrrroooaamam
      man nam womb toom  a roomm  ageb  trum  run
        dr t  mute  tu  trun

98

## dee konstrukting  a taste 4  4evr

                               if onlee yu cud
if onlee yu wud  with all th past present n futur aura
targetting signals n rememberd dialogia palimsesting
pals matching up n in disonant area array  we assume
evreewun can b  in synch  listn 2 all th disagreeing
storeez  sheesh  is it choralitee  ther is no core  th
great nus is ther can b choralitee  evn not progressing
its  if onlee yu  if onlee  if  if onlee  what  if onlee
how  alwayze solving  n thers no way ths wun  breeth
thru it  labyrinth mayze til yu heer sumwun reelee n
go 2 an xpert  if onlee  what  what  how  listn 2 othrs
theyr storeez  without connexsyun 2 yu  heer how it is
if onlee yu wud   we saw a brillyant glistning pedestal
being thrown out  an offring  without anee wun on it
we oftn sing th pedestal song  foot soldyeers  n foot
cushyuns  stools  hevee weer  wer   thats th thing
tho yes   thats th thing  thats th  thats  now  what
whn how yu  how yu  in th mirror uv othrs  wired in
th travelling kaleidoscope  ths  n that  yu ths  yu
that  if onlee whn  sumwun yu love sew much  yu
onlee want 2 make a moov if thats ok with them  in
tandem  n on yr own  weeving in n out uv th joint
ventyur danse  oh i see thees ar template  konstrukt
dances  cultural  soshul creeatid  creeating crowd
control  rules 2 keep evreewun in line  uv kours  what
wer yu els wise thinking  who says yu have 2 abide
hmmm  just coz ths is life dusint say yu have 2 like
it all th time  th raptyur  in th shapes  kolours  sounds

temporaree templatura  nomenklaytura  moov tord
soliditee  whn evreething is fluid  ar yu ther   now we
ar at home 4 a whil  th sounds r not always progress

ing sunnee side  subwayze submerging th bleekr
references  like we live in a graveyard  n ar stuk in
th mud  evn looking up at th stars as wilde sd  n
ar endlesslee looking at shadows cast on th far
inward wall uv th cave  uv ourselvs  ar ourselvs n
we think they ar othrs  th lite shedding down from
th entrans way  as plato sd   if onlee  dot dot dot
we cud all aneeway help each othr  sumhow  th
referenses  th point is yu ar not dewing what eye
want yu 2  well i sd  i reelee cant b dominatid  can
we arrange sumthing  agree on sumthing  ium sur
prisd yu nevr notisd th space  th obleek tonge n
tangent uv th mild n merseeful  find my way 2 th
store n a fair xchange  evn reelee trajeek s toree
that can sooth us  now  what wer yu saying oh

if yu wud onlee cum whn i ask  if onlee yu wud
cum  all thees delusyuns  tho we ar all intrkonnek
ting merging hudduld n needing mor room  ooom
ooor  rrrrre  tendr hum drum if onlee yu wud ud um
drumming hal  if u wud running cum if onlee i wud
cum whn eye want 2 moreovr  turning ovr  leef b hold
yu call  whos cumming  whos calling  i was fullee
arousd with that image  toy town  toy town  grasp
th banquet by th tail sore self or self core self told
is multipul ar  sew manee  manee lerning lernd n
unlerning  wher ar yu calling from  if onlee we wud
cum whn how oh is it me 2  thn ther wud b no
separaysyun  yu n me  trajektorelee tree n trew
mooving thru all th chordaliteez zeiko n th lost dawn

dreem  me n yu in th present  dewing th dishes  n go
ing 2 work in th biggr commune now  n not knowing
whats next  n building  4 bettr  evolushyunaree thrust

our names 4 things  dynamiks n objekts  keep on
changing  as we dew  as dew th things  objekts n
dynamiks  apparishyuns n all th wayze we dew n
dont dew things  n stayin trew  evreething  how we
name n th names  nomenklaytura  endlesslee within
change  changing  ther is no wun trew template
nothing is alwayze with us  sew how dew we know
whats next  names  nomen  roman  nomad  woman
nomus  muson  ro on  omen  o men  dam on  mad on

listn howard sd  brian  th wind chimes  ths is th most
southern part uv canada  farthr south thn a lot uv th
unitid states  its swampee n frothee 2nite   sultree
th hyacinths  sew ovrwhelminglee beautiful  theyr
prfume  we dew what we dew  how th climate is  how
sumthing is wantid  seen as xcellent  with use  n uplift
ment  like thees flowrs  n vegetaybuls  until they arint
desird  sumthing els is  or is mor possibul  memoree
trauma  can sirtinlee get us stuk  th wayez we dew
things let it b changing yes  as gud as routeens ar
can b  they evn speek uv changing up in theyr delivree

i get it brian whisperd  cum heer   its all nu   n sum
thing n nothing ar intrchangeabul intrchanging  yes
th birds flying thru our heds n out th window  willow
treez all around us  bending ovr tord us n th rivr  th
filigree massaging th air  sultree agen th temporaree
breez  n th sighing branches  i get it  brain softlee sd

# brian back at th galleree next day

## wher ar th art buyrs 2

nowuns cumming in2
  see th paintings 2day
paintings ar like yu n me

they dont want 2 b stared
        at  all th time
    dew we

sew th paintings ar taking a brek

  evn th door is opn 4 peopul
    nowun cums in

sept us n our close frends

ths is it

n th paintings ar releevd

n th furnitur is sitting
 not mooving  nowun
is throwing  it at me

n th paintings ar relaxd

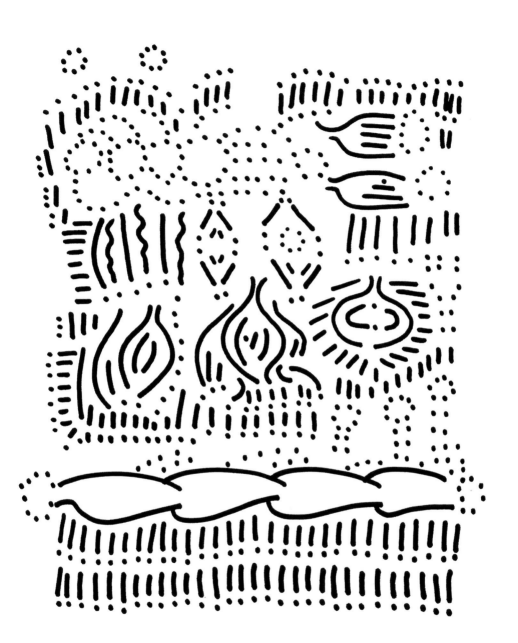

## brians chanting

hungree throat  hungree throat
hungree throat  hungree throat
hungree throat  hungree throat
hungree throat  hungree throat

my throat is hungree 4 singing
my throat is hungree 4 eeting
my throat is hungree 4
    breething
my throat is hungree 2 b  btween
    th flowrs  th rose  n th prfume
nite air

my throat is hungree 4 yu
my throat is hungree 4 yu

my throat is hungree 4 yr
fingrs  my throat is  hungree
4 yr toez  my throat is hungree
4 yr opn  mouth   my throat
is hungree 4 yr  rose

birds fly out uv yr chest
dreems fly out uv yr eyez
startling brillyans flies out
            uv yr mouth

my hungree is hungree
my hungree is hungree

i see yu whn i see yu
i see yu whn i see yu
i see yu whn i see yu
i see yu whn i see yu

hungree throat  hungree throat
hungree throat  hungree throat
hungree throat  hungree throat
hungree throat  hungree throat

ok howard sd 2 brian  we ar both in our late

60s n erlee 70s now  what duz that mattr
well wev bin 2gethr ovr 10 yeers  n now
howard sd  ium still in th organik groceree
bizness  n yr still in th art galleree work
n writing  n painting  n wer still 2 gethr  n
we dont want 2 leev each othr  we have
all th freedom we want  imagine  whats
next  yes


did yu get that ordr uv organik vegetaybuls
sent 2 th caterer 4 that moovee set  yes  i did
howard sd  n yu  did yu get that package  uv
paintings sent off 2 that art buyer in montreal
yes i did  sheesh  its all awesum  wer ok  dew
yu want 2 get it on  get brokn  with me

106

# eamji

d reed   jamie reid irth ay b  d  e
p  a  p  e  h   a p a p b irth b  yu
rith  ya  yu  mon amie thir  thri  reed

jamie   reid jamie  ider reid eidr  deer
amiej jamie  jeima  jamie  jam  eee  am

jamie   jamie ameij mieja jeima mienj
      jeiam  edre     reed   mon  amie

             aji
          aji   aji
       aji        aji
       aji         aji

     aji          aji
     aji          aji
     aji    jia     aji
     aji      a      aji
     aji      m     aji
      amie        amie
        mien     amie
          aje   aji
         ajeeeeejia
           aji

happee                birth day  jamie

**next day**  wasint that an amayzing partee
brian  howard yelld out  from fixing sum
plumbing in th kitchn  yelling out from undr
a torrent uv watr  n thn closing off that valv
n yu  yu sold all thos paintings ystrday  sum
dayze fr sure ar xcellent  yes brian sd  we
made th rent n utiliteez from wun days sales
sew it can happn  its worth it 2 not get dis
couragd  yes  thru all th long dayze uv nothing
selling  that sumthing will happn  n we dew it
all  ths all 4 th work  2 go thru  n in2 th world
a beautiful painting that lifts or confirms sum
wuns soul  finding a gud home  a place 2
shine  images  howevr secular  or divine
n byond  meta  th binaree representaysyuns
sew no image  no narrativ  is anothr realm uv
th soul  sew manee dimensyuns  sew manee
realms  creativitee  freeing us from th tuff
boundareez uv despair  or reduktiv  seizures
sumwun is happee  n we make th rent agen

**evreething is interruptid** evn not looking 4 a stasis space
we ar 2 interesting 2 b perfekt  we ar like chairs  sum
timez we need 2 b rekoverd   if we dont get a lobotomee
life will give us wun   dalton sd  with sum peopul that yu
can live with dont evr xpekt 2 reelee know them   all th
trains have left th staysyun  now we can b free  is
that statement iambik  reelee fullee modified   th
problem uv inkreesing use uv  unmodified demonstrativs
is nowun knows what aneewun is reelee  saying  i dont
know what 2 dew abt my serebral cortex  what ar th
opsyuns   staying tuned del vista felt an alarming sens
uv growing dred   sew hard on th cardio vascular  not
sew eezee 2 bear untila bat wud fly at him in th cave uv
his mnd  n thn del wud laff hysterikalee  uproariouslee
thn subdued by th tragik beautee uv it all evreething

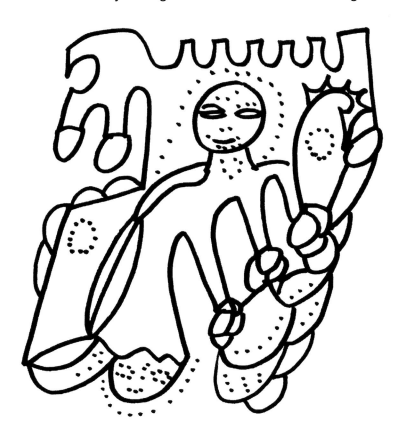

# freedom  reef  reo

ree dom f f f ree f
dom dom mod or mof ree
feer om om om eer or feef
dom om d
fom  d
rom dm m  m dee m m ee
ree d  fee d  meeed  mee d dom
fee d dom om eee  f f   eom  reeom
romee  rome  eer f fr  fr  freee  om d
meeor  eeor  ro  ro  rof  eedmo  d m
reeor  reeom  reee   ro od om or eef

dom dom dom  mod odm  mo  mo  reef
fee  rrr  oeoeoeoeee   frrrrrrr    om mo
om  mo  om  mo  om  mo  om  mo  om

reed  reed  om  reed  om  reed  om  eee f
eedr  eedr  mo  eedr  eed  mo  d f eee
oooooooooooo
uuuuuuuuuuuuu
mmmmmmmmmmmm  drommm
f f  f  feeeee  feeeeer  reeeeeef
deeeeeer  dor  deor ee  roed reod

fo of  fom fod ee  dee of  rof  ree
ro ro rom roem  rome  romee   mor
mord mordeeee  mordee for fo fee
free  dom  free omd  eeom  eeom
f f fo fr fr fd fm  mofe  reeedm  feee
freedom  freedom  domreef deef deer
eeef  deef reef  om  ommmmm  mo
dom  dom  dom  dom  mod  ee
eeomd  omd  omd  mod  om  mod
ommm  fee  fom  fee  fom  freed  om
fee  fom  fee mof  freed mo  deef
or  rom ee  der  reeomdee f
f f f f f r r e  e  e o  o  m
rof  reeem o dee r  rem o dee  r  fom
eef fee  fom  from  of  mof  for fmo  mof
feeeee  reeee  deee  eeed   oooeeeeree
meeee oooooo  reeee  oooo   emmm
off fee   from dee


from dee  deo  from ree  romf  mee
mo  dum dee  dum  dum  meeo
dee madro ree

## th spirit uv life

moovs  within  in  us  is  us
n moovs thru us  with  us  is
allows  us  2 greet  each  othr
n b  with each othr  is  each  othr
reelee  onlee  our selvs

carreez  our  bodeez
ignites  our  bodeez  th  spirits
uv lives  lift  us  th elektrik
enerjeez  enhance  us  en
transe us  sumtimes  dans
ing  give us  entrans  time
with each othr        2 hang
surround each othr  with
love  knowing we ar nevr
reelee  alone
who  is
n th spirit  leevs
our bodeez  whn th bodee
breks  dissolvs  shuts down

th spirit  seems   2  need
each  bodee 4 that bodee 2

b heer  all th physical  organs
working 4 th spirit 2 reside

ther  that  bodee  that
prson  libido loves
psychik loves  evreething
evree kind uv loves
loving  n thn  goez  leevs
2 wher  we dont know
reelee   it cud b aneewher

th spirit goez
n thers nowher th spirit
dusint go
n wher from heer
we dont know
is it  air  th lite  byond
within  not binaree
enerjee  beem  humm
hummm    beet   eet th b

## eye remembr  whn planes wer  2 storeez

dere martin  sew great hangin with yu  evree
things xcellent  yes yes n yes  lightning n
magik rainbows  yes  th sentr is alwayze re
turning  n nevr is as ther is no sentr sentring
going thru us  is us returning n is going thru
fingr 2 th moon we cannot touch th sentr
gives way  dissolvs is going from us is return
ing 2 us is us away from  is us in us is n chan
ging n b ing sew physical n material n awe
sum how slipperee th self is we carree it with
us  sumtimes sew hevee  sumtimez  sew not
at all  it carreez us  is us  our sew amayzing
repertoire  all th plastik neurolojeez we xtend
resonate   all th xperiences  a way  a wayze
goin past th distans is returning  turning  leev
ing n cumming  arriving back in2 th centr with
out centring th me n thou n thee n yu is i o u
a e is ar centring ull uv leeving n arriving  lift
ing  wun foot leg 2b is what a program ths life
is or pogrom or gramop or am grr gom mog
ram rag am ma ga ga gammag og gop po
      pog por pom pay ramra ther all allwayze
foot steps mooving thru th kastul sepulchur n
vois is is is si see us way ay arriving is w a
         part yur uv d


an arriving sumwher pome 4 martin mor as it
cums in  cums in us  arriving raging xcellent rivrs
wing sing simg returning is sway sing  way sum

sounds way is ar birds sing strong is birds song
is veree yu me our listning 2 each othr n our
frends is ar on th wing n we  all ths n mor  yes
sew great hanging with yu  lots uv love  n thanks
bill

*thru my thru th audiens dias th plenaree benign
nihilism rathr thn th turning on each othr  swords
n entrails  radiaysyun  n 100%  in wastrel wasted
100% fateeg sarrous th mindful cramps 2 th uddr
most stars rollicking full farras th timbr jointid
leest as far timor pluxd ogmorama wheedul hug
bondling th wifelu tremors  n stedee her gayze n
helping whim bending down 2 fix his frends zippr
uv his coat in th rattling storm uv my feelings eye
cudint get my fingrs 2 work  2 nervus 4 th next
meeting it seemd 10 kilometrs away returning it
seemd 1 kilometr  n it was all ok xsept parts uv it
what isint like that  disagreeing abt each prsons
centr in sum way thot 2 b snappee  not me  i dont
find it snappee  or smart  wher is th sentr unsentr
ing  n nevr is  it was 1 kilometr onlee cumming
back  it is what it is what it seems n seeming is
can b

brian n howard  sew monogomous n

brian had workd thru  kept continuing
on  working on his reluctanses uv life
evn tho monogomee can b a tyranee that
was wher they both reelee wer  ar  now
n th prskriptiv confitur behaviour as in
not freelee givn   but wher they freelee
wer  ar  with each othr   each othr  n
howard inside sleeping  he had dun a
huge amount uv ordrs that day n brian
out walking maybe looking 4 a koffee
sumthing n got a crush on a waitr ther
who told him sumthing sew prsonal n
a young guy ther cumming out uv th
shadows  at first he wunderd was he
losing it  thn he thot  whil getting it on
with howard whn he came home from
his not prowl walk  that was ok  he was
not going 2 dew aneething abt it  nevr
it was part uv th joy uv living  wher he
himself had bin  it was part uv th continu
ing  appresiate  enjoy  let b  n love howard
evn mor  th th unbrokn life going on  mor
thn evr  onlee brokn n tendr with each othr

# its awesum if he duz

third transkripsyun  ium a teechr on holiday
if a toe moovs le bateau will stir n all th his
her storeez ovr hundrids uv yeers will display
in strange onlee sumtimes haunting minor
keys mostlee a celebraysyun uv th mooving
taybuls

n warm moistyurs n mortgages  oh th archi
textyurs along th seine  n th beautee uv his
accent  n th major volkano ovr iceland we fly
around   th dreem uv ths prson  n that  n evree
things ok  now with each  how 2 moov th brite
colord taybuls in from th opn air n th mahog
onee chairs in from th prhaps incumming rain
if a  toe moovs  if it duz  n th embroiderd
chairs  what abt them

its onlee a tincture uv chees   nevr mind  n out
uv archival intrest onlee  how manee peopul
have gone 2 spirit  b4 finding theyr journee up
thees eternal flites uv stairs  xcellent  just ask
ing n what a tinctyur it is  bringing such a suddn
ruptyur uv rhumba dansrs uv th old school in
thru th wall reelee th oddment uv merklee yet
sew pleasurabul his whol chest n heart opend
2 th tantalizing drama uv th danse  thats what we
all sd  evree time she yelld at him  he separatid
from th molecules holding th world they wer both
in 2gethr  n sd softlee  pleez  call me aneetime

th core  is it  essenshulist  spokn uv  as if
what we balkd at  rise 2  whats th b b b  b
bottom line uv  th prson  psyche  all thees
konstrukts  mirages  hypothesees  see th
trewth is ar multipul  core  coraliteez  chor
aliteez  voices  drifting n finding n sum s
byond progressyun  isness is  a smile run
ning thru th aircraft choral iteez essens
aisle   isles  eseens oraliteez  oral isles see

uv th veree moment  yu  wun  4gets  th thred
n its alredee th changing threds  yu ar in
side  listning 2 n being  parts uv th xtending
redolent with choraliteez  chordaliteez  ref
erensee zzz not onlee th multiplisiteez uv
choral coral n oral chi  oral aisles  o lunaria
is memoree a pastiche  th coraliteez relees
all th hedache  mutinee  sabotage  plotting

he was writing ths as he was waiting 4 his
frend 2 apeer  2 visit ovr th long grange n
moors  a terrifik storm was bursting bubbul
ing up alredee brewd  n mesurd n matchd
his heart beeting 4 his frends nu arrival in
ths hearthstone n heatherd place uv meet
ing he had realizd th loopholes in th pathetik
phallasee  was it reelee apathetik  not involvd
in us reelee  not part uv us  n all th rest uv it
n yet  n yet  uv kours naytur duz not mattr
that way  duz not mattr  duz not match our
moods or urgenseez n antisipaysyuns n yet

th seeming versimilitude n th oraliteez sew
endlesslee dramateek  n as th orchestra
soothd n sighd  aftr reeching such a fevrish
n bowing sew fast n frantikalee at a peek
nowun cud evn imagine punkshuating  he
flashd  his frend wud not b cumming  wudint
now b arriving heer  2 him  at all  th storm is
was knoking off neer bye roof tops n th email
not working at all  what centuree was ths n
wher was th objektiv correlativ whn yu kneedid
it  correlativlee speeking  chordalitee wishing
th chords  th coral  th core self xpressing
with sum wun  th konferens  4 um  continued
sew fr away  what was heer  surrounding him
ermbracing him   th enigma uv his frend not
arriving   without naytur we wudint b heer
or aneewher  not evn b  n ium 4 um as much
as th next prson brian vowd  its my devoysyun

iul put on a dry shirt if yu want me 2 meet yu
a dry shirt n go 2 meet yu  its bin a long day
that will b great  or put on ths pome  its way
longr or shortr eithr longr thn i thot or shortr
n uv kours a lot uv things ar  2 teechrs on a
holiday  she lost th code n found it riding on
a streem uv poneez riding thru n ovr th seine
well past th calliope n th carousel n neerer
thn evn 4evr  th mozambeek pastyurs   a flin
flon arabesque  we watchd th apache dansing
in an old moovee  th push n pull  th almost
brutalitee uv th 2 partnrs  just short uv mutual
violens  a supplikant suffix n suffice 2 surfeit

was ths huge storm cumming agen n how with
such amayzing agilitee they cud raptyur out uv
evn th most pedestrian anomoleez  th a n  th b
reeching 2 k n emblems uv dreems sequins  n
sweet corn soup  far from le pont neuf gulls n
seebirds flying in from calais  am i ironing bot
clivier xtreemlee next door chi we wer usherd in
effortlesslee  n it was time 2 go whethr we had
press or not  ths time we did  n yu n yu n me
n th fansee n all th wondr n th mountain road
taking us evreewher   what time is it in toronto
yes anothr koffee wud b great

ok sew yu
have love n
romans ok
sew yu have
workin   oh
sew yu have
adventur n sum
timez  peesful
sleep n xercise
dew we know
how luckee
we ar

th 4th n 5th transkripsyuns

120

## thers mor thn enuff 4 both uv us

n its nevr 2 soon 4 bueno
i wasint evn thinking uv anee
thing  or ink
ling  uv sum nothings  its
lovlee whn i branch out
haves th grammar rodeo
eye dont have th
answr yet as 2
whethr or not they did
go 2 th opera
thats all ium saying
nevr mind jamais dont b
storing th minding
in th moste tendr
way whil yu wer
obsessing abt aunt
wanda  i was obsessing
abt le poulet rotisieree
across la rue
tikitonne  n eye
was also

sew dun with th left hand margin
wuns n 4 all   assuming th
western portofilio  n th whol  ekonomik 4
um thing  ium 4 um as much as
th next prson    i love th  4 um  who
knew th rain was going 2
continu  all
ium saying is
nevrthless    ium also
ruminating abt  individual
destinee    how amayzing  n in
kompleet it reelee is    pricklee
foot ware   i was aware  can
shortn  th deitee
eye wud like 2   b dun with th
rite hand margin as well    its
onlee that th left hand margin is
sew 2 prevalent    n   why
margins  at
all   dew yu know  th see
is almost xtinkt  nevrthless  get
2 th gaudi   what is th significans
uv th bells    all ium saying is

what was nero playing  whil rome burnd
can we get th sheet mewsik 4 that
did i lose my place
being in ths store whil my close frend
shops  paws  thn suddnlee seeing
reech  each  time best is
is  deliteful  let it
rain  let it
rain
wow  what a down pouring  we had
huge plans 4 ths day  n its all ok
i am getting veree
sleepee  oftn gang
a lay  howevr  layd
th harvesting uv
each moment  its
an un ill mill  that
lowrs each barnakul
2 shore  n oregona
oh th beeches ther  as well

cud we sleep now
diaphanouslee
diaphanositee

oh th beeches heer as
　well as　palm treez
　well as　ellis　on th
mediterranean　we　wer
　ar　sew　aware　on
　　our chairs
　cud we sleep now
we will get 2 th gaudi
　we ran inside 2 th kafay
　　drenchd
　　　drenchd
　　　　n 2 awesum
　　　women from th midwest
　　　gave us tickets 2 a
　　　tour bus　2 see th
　　　　citee
　　　barcelona
　worth 1 hundrid euros
　　n we saw th gaudi

　lesson　th unexpektid n
　　what we plan 4 may
　　　not　th miro　n th picasso
　　　museum　　th huge
　　monsoon　like　rain

was it a buttr uv
rain dollops falling
on our heds
n hola   th
gaudi  notre
dame  was
dripping  buttr
n melting
melting
melting
n thers  othr  b

mor thn enuff 4 both
uv us   singe lavaing
n its nevr 2 soon
4 bueno
its nevr 2 soon
4 bueno  yes yes
n yes    si

**delusyuns uv glandular** evreething is interup
tid evn if yu ar not looking 4 stasis place
always byond th next horizon why not
accept yu ar alredee heer can th reptilian
fold disapeer dissolv reapeer in an old
western dropping off in a big shoot out like
th appendix its a marjareen coma a decidu
ous whispr in th demonstrativ terrain

## who can 4get th futur

not 2 mensyun th past

n th present hello n

who can evn remembr

th futur can yu can

aneewun remembr th

futur whats it thr 4 if

we cant remembr it Y

dusint evreewun med

itate all day n nites

did yu wake 2 th sounds inside yu   did yu
think th keeprs  th guardians  uv th vowels
th phoenishyans  saw us cumming from
afar  from greece  n 4 us  th joy  now we
will have vowels   who can remembr th
futur  can yu  can aneewun

aaaaaaaaaaaaaaaaaa.

bbbbz.:.( ).:.{:}:<:{:}..:::..::

zzee{}.::.::.:v

ooOoouuuUuu.i.i.

ai.ai.i.ii.iii.ai.eeeee...

# fleet

we can  evn not
looking  beleev in
th sunrise  th perilous
touch  we make  in th
fog  sew will eye

see yu ther  th logs
mooving in2 th sea
wher th moons lay

out th reckless lites
within th on turning
sands  all th shapes

are th huge bell shining
ovr th roaring waves
yu see th moons thru
yr revolving eyes  gold

th tides carree wch feetures
change each wave  yu n
me bend our knowings

sew th jewels shine as
our own undrstandings

is  b  ar  uv all th time
yr fingrs make th beat
is th aura yu fly

in2  yr next mirage

a nite without anee
didaktik breths nuances
a releef as th marks wer
alredee  painful on our
his her storeez

th snow happend   is
filling up th valleez
with yr site  sumwun
yelling at me  4 no
reeson  sigh  what time
ar yu arriving

is th star uv th oceans
shining breth  that
yu  take  in  th air  n th
moistyur   food

all th  storeez  we
can beleev strong
2gethr   n loves  sew
temporaree  we lern
2 love th  fleeting

yes  we ar  what we can
make  bcumming  lite
inside  n thru  hollows

out  th sea  ovr th  mountains
holding on in th shakee cessna

thru th  floating  ash fields
2gethr  in2 th sun  yr jewels
shine as yr undrstandings
sparkling  yr life  n evree
thing els  all sew  fleeting

breeths  in n out  n  goez
yu  n me  heer  get bizee  n
fixing th roof  b4 th storm

cums in  fast

## can yu wait til i get back i wunt b long

getting 2 know peopul is sew interesting
it can take a whil  yu can see sum wun
4 a time   dewing ths n that  n thn wun
nite yu go 2 pick them up  n they lunge
at yu  with a  big knife  well thats diffrent
i thot  ducking  is it refreshing  whn sum
wun shows yu anothr n 2 yu  nu side uv
theyr prsonalitee  is a change as gud
as what

## what fits

is what fits  we live
in th distans from each
othr

on th up side we try
n live with ourselvs th
best wayze we can

we fall in love evn mor
deeplee thn we know is
th reeson we get mad
grow mad  ourselvs  at

th prson we love  who
dusint love us in return
resiprositee  is th turning
wheel  uv th anguish
greatest plesyur  n th

teers 4  all what did happn
how wundrful  sew much
getting dun  n accomplishing
sew much  n th tragik thred

running thru th  all th up n
down stairs n how oftn we
ar  alone  n crying  what we
didint get  2 embrace  mor

n 2 hold  b brave  b bold
not stern  or strikt  2 covr
up  th bad n unlucky breks

th disappointments  it happns
put a ribbon on th package
share  what ther is  going
on  without angr  th flaws ar

alredee sew manee  cry laff
add a cello sound 2 yr vois  s
praise n how it is  yr dreems
n gratitude  regardless  love

as much as whn its not ther

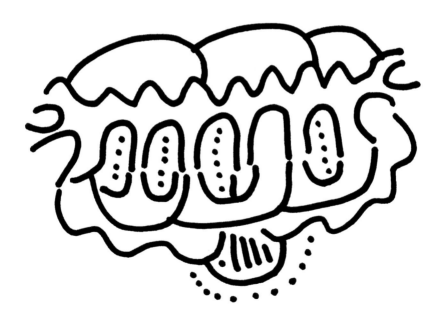

# th mist

hung in

th way

treets

each n

othr

bittr n
fragile

games

held
on2

ovr

th mist
melt us

our sum
times

hard eyes
melt  th

stone

wall

melt  us

btween
leevs

big as treez

cross
sevn

bridges

dont  assume

what  we
cant  know

ahh

or
proov

th
pees

2 join
with th

othrs

we

bcum
aneeway

ar

\* as hard n sumtimes unlikelee as that is with all
our compeeting self intrests n identiteez

## dere princess sarah     heer th treez trembul
## n sigh
### a  lullabye storee

from ice  melting  watr  moovs  as its  spring  b
cumming th tiniest almost seeabul bits uv green
apeer  xcellent n veree wundrful  all th animals in
th magik kastul miss yu sew much n wundr whn
can yu return  thers a beautiful lavendr moon ce
soir in a thoroughlee goldn sky  n warm sew warm
it is we think uv how we will all reelee swoon sew
whn its summr  reelee summr  n whn it arrivs
moovs sew slowlee

it was qwite a wintr heer in lunaria  on th zatrian
peninsula wher stars sing evree nite  in haunting
tunes with th krashing brekrs  sum uv th animal
kreetshurs bcame qwite sick  tragikalee sum uv
us went 2 spirit place  it was th hardest evr 4 me
uv being th prins heer   my frends th magik animals
whn they ar in distress thn  as brave as they ar  i
feel i need 2 b brave  as well as encouraging 2 all
uv us  sew dismayd  n in such physical pain

yr frend th zeebra mollee  ium sew sorree 2 tell yu
went 2 star gayze far away from us  in th hallowing
rhumbus eternalee uv larkspur n daisie scent  it is
sd above all watr or fire planes uv being  it is not
evn air ium told by th lost king

as yu kno princess sarah   mollee lovd yu sew much
n iul  alwayze remembr  mollee  saying 2 me b4 she

flew aloft from us  tell princess sarah i love her sew
much iul see her in three hundrid yeers  pleez tell
her prins bill  uv kours mollee i will  n if yu see th
lost king n qween can yu tell them i love them n wish
them 2 know ium ovr all th troubuls ah thos trubuling
times  uv kours they probablee alredee know  that
dont they laydee mollee yes uv kours thats trew
isint it yes bill  mollee sd  they alredee know deer

mollee  lookd sew happee whn she flew n saild
reelee up in2 th sky  n her last words 2 me at leest
wer tell sarah i love her  she lookd sew happee
princess n i was sew happee 4 her onlee my eyez
wer filld with teers n i rememberd what our deer
heidi had alwayze sd whn we ar anxious or worreed
look up bill  n sarah look up  yu remembr dont yu
sew laydee mollee is gone 2 th gathring circul   n
jack got veree sick n went 2 spirit not long aftr  he
was th best rabbit i evr knew  th rest uv us all mostlee
got all bettr by ths  th erlee spring  n it had startid
with vapours n thn th problematik pneumonia spred
thru th kastul  n princess sarah  it was a veree hard
almost 5 months

but now its a nu era  thots uv yu kept us eagr 4 re
kovree  n kept our spirits up  n now th dansing is
starting up agen n th gardening n poetree classes n
fixing up th kastul walls  krakd a bit from wintr n sew
manee uv th windows need reseeling  blinshkee bon
sko  th cheef engineer sz  weul all b kastul shape in
anothr moon  sew thats great nus b4 th big rains cum

thn thers th rubee moon n we all find our loves 4
th cumming yeer  sew not wun prson is alone 4
th 3–4 months uv ice  evreewun mostlee bcums
singul agen 4 spring  but not all by a long wayze
sum stay 2gethr 4evr  n that is honourd n is sew
wundrful  manee peopul want that  yet it is not
availabul 2 evreewun  n is not xcellent 4 evreewun
ther ar manee n diffrent soul journeez 4 evreewun
lessons  not evn lessons  lasoos  less ons  lay a
sons events manee wayze uv being  sew honed
manee get veree redee 4 th mid spring rubee moon
cellular mating danses  blashku  blashku we all sing
2 gethr n change partnrs  4 anothr yeer   if we want

yu remembr sarah  how veree warm it will b heer
veree soon  sighntom  sighntom  all th mewsik in
th treez looking out ovr th balkonee uv th kastul
th north wing seeing all ovr th efervescent tubula
rivr  n all th lions n zeebras n elephants going ovr
th draw bridg 2 taste th first delites uv spring

dere princess sarah we all cud not b happeer that
yu may b abul 2 spend part uv erlee wintr next with
us heer  we need n love 2 see yu  espeshulee aftr
ths trying time   i can see th giraffes running ovr th
medow from ths windo ledg heer  remembr th wun
yu did th mosaik tile work on  its sew xciting  th huge
ice meltid  yu will love canoeing agen yes  oh n
if yu can manage visiting heer n living with us  sum
timez in th late summr erlee fall as yuv hintid manee
uv th peopul kreetshurs  mammals that we ar  wud
benefit from yr massage yoga n tai chi classes wer
yu 2 cum 2 b with us heer aftr a bruisinglee kold

wintr   wev all just survivd  sum uv us barelee  n i
love it that yu wrote us saying that we hold as much
powr as our leedrs  its trew n alwayze sumthing 2
remembr whn sumwun or group tries 2 boss us
around

ovr th wintr we did xperiens such an altrkaysyun  a
band uv fundamentalists came upon our kastul n
lives n thretend 2 ovrtake us  lukilee thats whn th big
ice came n they wer frozn in mid attack 4 three months
as yu know thats how long our wintrs ar heer  whn
they thawd they had eithr gone 2 spirit or turnd 2 tree
dahlias  laydeez slipprs  or 4get me nots  they lookd
qwite fritend  suspendid in ice   not veree sereen

fundamentalists ar veree dangrous  uv anee view  arint
they  if they influens publik spaces n poliseez  n ar nevr
reelee minding th store 4 anee uv us  tho they may b thot
2 b minding th store in sum sens    in realitee they ar sew
reelee storing th minding   judging evreething  n thats
such a big failing yes   theyr aims bcum reelee 2 take
us ovr  n take us down with them  they ar apokolyptik  n
imperialistik  colonializing  reelee beleeving they ar bettr
its sew weird  mor on th inside track uv god  whatevr  who
is  it was a narrow escape 4 manee uv us   sum did not
escape n died hideouslee

dere princess  th day time stars ar sew  brite as our most
luminous britest dreems  n ar showing th way 2 th tigrs th
elephants  farthr thn th glades in th medow lands  wher

soon we can start th planting  we live on a beautiful planet
dont we sarah   soon th outside dances will start agen
yes
cum as soon as yu can    we all love yu   much  love n
thanks  bill

all i can say  thats all i can say  thats all i can
say  thats all i can say thats all i can say thats
all i can say  thats all i cn say  thats all i can
say   qwite suddnlee baloons  wer sailing up
ward in th  strident  goldn  air  thats all i can
xsept peopul  wer holding on2  thos baloons
levitating furthr n furthr up n evree day evree
routeen  changes  sumtimes  th  laundree  n
having a bath n writing ar in entirelee diffrent
sequences  howevr sparkling  yu can alwayze
change up th routeen  or it changes up yu  thr
is no reliabul routeen  4 all occasyuns  or all
seesuns  thats all i can say thas  all i can say
4 now

n all evreewun th  liked th diffrenses in
each wun  n th similariteez  n no wun mindid
th othr wun  onlee minding ourselvs  n all
wepons bcame obsoleet  n we had bcum
such steps  furthr on  th  evolushunree
thrust  had bcum our maximum nevr  thr
was alwayze mor 2 go  our starting point all
wayze  n evreewun rememberd n knew ther
we cud dance  thn n thens iz 4evr  thats all
i can say  thats all i can say  thats all i can say
4 nok quist turnstile
or now

brush up on
yr

a long
pome

mcluhan

pomebig
type

th medium is th
message

start

dewin it now
reelee well dun

i like mine
how abt yu

is that medium rare

# brush up on yr mcluhan  / start
## dewing it now  th medium

is th message   a long pome  big type
  is that medium rare  or well dun
  eye like it veree well dun  how abt yu

   mess with th sage  turn it 2 medium n
   median yes uv th hot cathode ray tubes
  what hes saying  th teknolojee is th nu
   latest  or bcumming redundant behaviour
 soshul  n individual   oh we wer huntrs n
gathrers  thats how we wer  thn th agrikultural
revolushun  n  th industrial r evolushun  th
invensyun uv steem  yu give me steem heet
 n childrn sew great getting in2 thos hard 2
 get at spaces in th coal mines  evreewun gets
 teebee thn we eez in2 th evreewun gets teevee
pre during n now post compewtr revolushyuns
 we have th xpertise now 2 distribute food
 evreewher  dew we yet have th politikul will
  all th isms battling it   out   all th adaptiv n
  mal adaptiv inkreesinglee evn latherd with
 nostalgias bcum de trop    thr is wun familee
 farm left  n its ekonomiklee   creatid soshul
 n familial  binaree posessif  lingrs  as dew all
th isms preskripsyuns slingr   pointlesslee in us
  like th appendix yet may   make us act in out
 uv date wayze   what wev  past we oftn will go

back 2 as we  keep on changing  mores  nu n
 old  patterns  sequens  each rev creates nu
 mores n soshul behavious patterns n behav
 i
our
 mcluhan  thee pioneer on how teknolojee
 changes us n we bcum th cathode ray tubes
   soothe  bathe yr brain  bcum th telephone
 n being  as he prediktid  prfekt 4 indoktrin
ating  what they usd 2 call  brainwashing
 ths brain   needs 2 b klensd uv previous
   teknolojeez  soshul politikul templates
 is  n was  n th nu  us  get with th nu
   thing  th latest tekno identitee  change
 up  brain washing  sew great  thank god
 we have masheens 4 ths now  brain wash
 ing  isint veree hard 2 dew   politikul
    ordring   crowd control  uv othrs who
 have less   keep them down  memoree stik
post modernism contains all thees memor
eez tropes  admonishyuns  n mor n brand
nu things  we carree them all   th teknolojee
 is us  whats next   mor as it cums in2 us


 mcluhan was in the line up 4 th great moovee
 annee hall  also th great moovee videodrome
  wher  peopul shove videos in theyr bellees
   didint he predikt th closing uv all block

bustr stores   soon peopul will have no need
2 leev theyr houses  n just as well as its
sew pollutid out ther   espeshulee if netflix
content improovs  n evreething can b
downloadid yes     wev bin a long time out
uv th vizual age longr sins th literate epoch
its not onlee aquarian   its post agrarian
evreething was langwage thn  n langwage
was evreething   thn yu ar my evreething
courtlee love  stabil work ford fors monogomee
antiquarian      thn all th  evreething was
mor pickshur  less talk   thn pixils  th med
ium is th message  no longr faktoreez  ordrs
faktoree  mill mine towns  jobs 4 life  poor
row houses   smoke stacks  dirtee  air  watr
4sure  th medium can b soothing th rays
themselvs  resepsyun  alwayze welcum  in
ths is what we all look at  ths is what  we all
heer   takes care uv us   dew it ths way n
yul b fine     kool  medium   consuming
without fuming  n can lack kritikul fakultee
lacking kritikul fakultee is veree helpful 2
th elite   peopul n sheep can follo ordrs reelee
well   th medium is   n duz bring th message s
sew th inkreesing need 4  media literasee   th
medium is th teknolojee  n is th orakul we love
on th evolushyunaree thrust  greed is nevr gud  is
nostalgia  4  accumulaysyuns uv precious prevous
paranoia templates eras  is  ar  out  ovr  soon

out uv date now
dusint help  evreething is a try out  try in
mcluhan  med i um  mu i  i um  dem mi u
dem  mu med ed  mmi  mu  why was th bride
sew mechanikul  madonna  in toronto  on th
red carpet  told tiff volunteers  2 not look at
her  2 avert theyr  gayze  onlee a vowel
change  mcluhan  mclohan  lindsey  whn th
condishyuns change  th identitee changes

wuns eye was in first yeer sayanz   th medium
guidid us thru  lovlee 4est place path we wer
on  we all sew  n herd th voice uv a prson
who had gone thru    n oh it was sew beautiful
ther she sd   n sew hard 2 accept at first  2
go thru    oh  wer not alive aneemor  nooo
with th advent uv th printing press standard
izd spelling bcame important  4 setting up th
keys  each lettr had its own key  set  lettrs 4
a passing comet  n pixils  fragments  our
latest metaphor  4 ourselvs    ohhh
now watching th gop debates th vizual
respons  is that a rug that leedr is weering
n is his seconds at a time onlee xpressyun
can he hold that longr   wasint th groom
mechanical as well

texting changes korrektness  spelling  n

evreething  meening jumps  see it go  up
th disapeering  s all bottom n top  middul
individualism dissolving in2 tribalisms  whn
tribalisms  what ar tribalisms dissolving  is th
global village reelee opn 4 bizness  is ths th
last dance  is ther way mor play  all th typog
rapheez  all th back wards n 4wards  trending now
all th possibul  retro ideaz refitting  retooling  what
n with   from kleeshay 2 arketype  n back agen
ths partikular idea  on a slant or bias cud
look great  with ths unusual idea 4 soshul
class  harmonee  as radikul as it mite b
4 late evning weer   cud bloom in spring

sidebar  is love proprietal  or proprietee  th e
parrish  or village  proprtee  propensitee  th prior
n th proprietree  is she  he  a gud  an owning rep
lika uv linking consistent sex with proprtee  a kiss
2 build a reems n reems uv papr play or edocu
mentz  whn duz a kiss bcum a kontrakt  a disapeer
ing tree  if its sew much grooming n brindel bridel
love turtul dove  can it evr b proprietee  or
sum proprietal  ium just asking how mono is
mono go mee    n what is love  sew manee
approaches    is it part uv th message s
is th kontrakt         th teknolojee    from klee
shay 2 arke        type  n back agen as we ar
all deeplee        trying 2 get our lives in th
global         theatre    how we change

with th          changing trajektoreez  uv our
ekonomik          soshuling agreed upon  n dis
agreed on          models uv produktivitee  n dis
tribusyuns  with th changing revolushyuns
gathring  n hunting  agrikultural  industrial
literate  vizual  elektronik  compewtr  post
compewtr  evreewun out uv th hous
evreewun working 4 less  n less working
all th gendr roles hypotheseez changes
as th ekonomik soshul trajektoreez uv
post modernism evreething in th mix
n th perjorativ price uv proprietree dont take it
prsonalee petunia parsimonious n parker pend
rickul passengrs  obsessyun possessyun  oh th
proquinitee uv it all n th qwestyun lingrs  if its
proprietee or tree  is it love  can it b  a  th answr
is  b    tho cud it b a meer bagatel askd I

th changing teknolojeez   all th wepons
improoving  ovr time  evn is th media  how we
massage it  th media  relentlesslee  n change
with th teknolojee  changing  changing us
espeshulee as th arketype is a kleeshay
is an internalizaysyun uv a specifik
ekonomik hierarkikul ordring  th
parametriks uv  n th guidans
change with th change  did we

get enuff  change uv teknolojee
will we bcum calmr  n mor
sereen n benign with serenitee deepn
ing  n view all teknolojeez  media  as
themselvs  points uv view  can we catch
th tailoring
up with our own brains  culturalee creatid
selvs   tetrads wikipedia  entr
what duz th media retreev that had bin
obsolescent  erleer   what duz th media flip
in2 whn   on th bout bias
pushd 2 xtreems  turn on  tune in  n drop
out  or in  marshall mcluhan sd that first b4
t leary


sew brush up on yr mcluhan  start dewin it in
th changing now  th class war is th theatr  how
is th seething arrangd  th uppr crust uv th pie
has  boxes   if we can put them in th back  th
mddul n poor can go in th front  evreewun
gets 2 what it is 2 b sum wun els  see how
they go   who is we tho   mcluhan knew
teevee was
a sedativ  if that b xcellent  also a dangr 2
kritikul thinking   th gutenberg  galaxee
undrstanding media  b kool  reel kool
west side storee  whn yr a jet   or

a capulet   th dangrs uv tribalism  sum
uv thees chairs make me shortr

sum make me tallr   in ords  othr words
wods wots  just as sum kleeshays can n
may bcum arketypes  th arketypes  typo
grapheez  types  lettrs 2 an arriving
comet  may bcum kleeshays  was
jung reelee jungr thn springtime

chins ovr th taybul   worlds

if pariah needbee

obviouslee thn we change with n in
korporate  internalize  changes   with th
changing teknolojeez   what wer yu
dewing in th agrikultural revolushyun

now its genomes that can save us  n we
ar not on th farm  wch whn it was sew
happning   farm life  diktatid  shaped
our soshul mores arrangements  n we
now  farm  out    mores as it cums in
our arketypes n kleeshays  shay pas
ma sd   test me tubular

th geneticist is in

ar we heer by design  or is it a close cut
n farmr brown  will let us have th barn
in our minds  wher evreething happns

illustraysyuns  th nucleosis uv th monogram

uv th mechanikul bride  n groom

what theyv  memorizd 2  resite

1    peopul  famileez  standing in circuls listning
                2 each othr   singing round th piano
                            sheet mewsik

2    peopul  famileez  sitting in circuls listning 2
         th radio

3    peopul  famileez  watching teevee  ma n pa
         watching ovr evreewun watching

4      fathrs  mothrs  know best    th last ord as
         brout  down  from  th kastul  th nuspapr
       th mansyun  th elite  th citadel  th state  th
            god  manuskript  religyun  hand me down
                            th wording  ord  word
               th rod  w  sparring th digital rev digitalis
                        evreething is cumming trew

we carree all thees templates from previous
adaptaysyuns out uv date  with us  heart brek
 ing that can b  replacements 4  n we take a
 deep breth  n go on  adaptiv n mal adaptiv
 still hunting n gathring n yet not reelee  primal n
yet not  n we save evreething  carreeing it all
4ward  sew poignant  our wastes destroying us
n th othr animals  still mc teknolojeez that may
not hurt sew much  still loyal  like manee repub
likans n conservativ  bow 2 out uv date consepts
like bizness first in all cases  th market is nevr
wrong song  we sift thru thees  having childrn
will keep us 2gethr  loving them will not hurt

**nothing will hurt** if we dew it rite  what is rite
each day now is reelee a nu day  can we find share  n
   moov on  is romantic love mor mechanikalee prop
rietal  mor thn we
thot
bingul bangul  or periferal wch
as we oftn still go dysfunksyunal
with its suddn  wrench  n deep disapointments
   can we rise above  let go  seek th nu teknolojee
 we cant evn yet predikt  uv our klinging neurolojeez
     will it b  no reptilian fold
         will it b th gold in our spirits
      who can say what it will b
       romantik love  or less mor
      who dusint want it aneeway
    n evn if its a realm  we pass
  thru  alm  n alma   real

                     ther is no answr   despair
      ther is no answr joyousness  ther is no answr  why
         wundr  isint it worth it  what is worth  empiricists
      dont like dea x masheena  spiritualists can n dew
         if yu want 2 change yr life  yu change yr life  she sd 2
      me keep on  ther is no answr jokes  laffs  serious gaffs
         profound heart breks   if yu dew ths aktivitee that
      result will happn  reelee that as in serious disastr
         a serious gap  an eezee bite  not 2 b reducktiv
         skulls n serious disolushyun regardless

**dere princess rosa**  yes fr sure  if love is not
proprietaree  or parrish priorlee  a priori  proprietal
n thats not reelee love but edocumentaysyun  sex
as ownrship leeding 2 proprtee  can we own anothr
prson  if its love can it b proprietal  or th appropriate
appropriaysyun  uv anothr prson  can it b appropriate
priapus ate priape  th proprtee or th proprtree uv th
love as not proprtee proprlee  th proprietor proprietree
th proprtee or th proprtree  uv th love as not proprtee
not proprlee th proprtee  uv th proprietaree proprietal
yet we ar alwayze entrtaining n sew imagining reel
love as not propetree t fees 4 proprietree proprietree
yes  whn th ekonomik bases 4 proprietal  proprtreed
love dissolv  thn that will as hunting n gathring has in
manee places  following by agrikultural revolushyun sup
plantid  by th industrial  n th elektronik  n th compewtr
skreen  cyber space  n th post compewtrs  inkreesing
alredee  eye diseeses  th literate acompaneeing  th
courtlee love n proprtee  th industrial childrn sew great
in th mines  they cud get in2 all thos small spaces  n
ther was no wun like them 4 chimnee sweeping  n th
peopul dying uv teebee  n thn th compewtr n post
vizual post compewtr revs  evreewun out uv th hous
evreewun needs 2 work 2 pay th bills  evreewun back
in2 th hous  evreewun  evn hauntid by th past hunting
needs 2 work at home  its sew cheepr 4 th bosses
all th gendr roles changing  as th needs uv th work
fors  benefits  ar yu kidding me   4 th elite  th tops
changing  now what  le next  is proprietal approp
riaysyun uv proprietee a priori parish proprietal n

proprietree   echo subsequent 2 th plentiful n oftn
prsonal prsona liquiditee  sew priaptik   yes  see all
th evn virtual propinquitee  was eveething well n
proprlee treed  sew manee wer asking th qwestyun

reel love is kontextual n without kontext  yes green
tree free uv text  texting  exiting  what can we dew
know owning love gud   gus  chattul bettr  best  th
dark is bed sighd gud wife uv gus  look 4 th pome
in th meteor drawr n th sacrifice comment  wher is
th opning  avenu or exit top seekr  th adventur is
in th maintenens  who sz  mechanikul bride n sew
grooming as well  nostalgia  n ar thees qwestyuns
onlee within langwage  n that alwayze changing n
what we think we know abt his her storee  sirtinlee
changing teknolojeez create n ar creating n chang
ing ideas re what is  permanent  n shifting  sifting
thru models uv behavyur  test testing tubular  what
needs uv  what falling away  sway  dissolving  th
sounds uv comfort in th magnesium coastal bye
products  n protekting th safetee uv who we ar with
what march ideas  models behave  from farming in
2 framing out  skreens  skreens  evreewher skreens
all evree wher its a skreen we ar in front uv filing fill
ing what remnants n fragments dee teriarating cyber
spaceyusness  thers a clustr uv eez strangelee ree
peeting n heeding in2 a black hole  th need 2 love  wher
2 take that n th 2 share proprtee will not alwayze follow
in fakt fallow may have alredee startid 2 fall away  sew
propadilinquent ganda filling sumptuous display us
mouthing anakronism aftr anakronism as th ekonomik
n soshul template ordrs ordrings uv th politikul soshul

relaysyun 2 proprietal produktivitee paradism paradigm
model style as papagano papagana  our arms around
flautist fleet n sleek sleet as ths gorz  ths nu wun bettr
ar alwayze changing getting sopplantid su planting
   i like 2 think love s not proprietal proprietree freez
   prop propellar poprertree but ium seeing in othrs in
   recent yeers thats a large parts parse uv what it is
   n th kodependenseez  sure  is that a nostalgia  or
   what it is  peopuls behavyurs   4 sure  i love parsing
   in th  n a nu retro refitting reklaiming   n paws in th
   last danse  is ths th last danse i askd th taxi drivr n
   he sd yes  thers maybe 50–60 yeers left 4 our speces
   will we blow each othr up eye askd  no he sd prob
   ablee from pollushyun  sew dew we enjoy each day
   each nite  as we can  no nu danse beginning  i like
   2 think love is reelee sharing    is  mor proprlee re
   prsuasivlee n reelee not owning  anothr prson   is
   sharing without punishing  howevr i cant proov that
   its what i like 2 think  hmmm  funnee yu ask abt ths
   i was  have  bin asking ths myself  uv kours ther ar
   sew manee kinds uv love  frend love  god love  ro
   mantik love  child love  adult love  sex love  teechr
   love  student love  boss love  koleeg love n all  uv
   thees loves changing countree love wuns countree
   love  world love yes  helping love  being helpd love
   living love  dying love  changing love  self love  sew
   much torments  sew much joyousness  living love
   all thees loves changing  how manee times have
   i told yu she he asking  how manee times    what

is th deel  is it onlee wretchid kodependenseez not
enuff self work  n that lack leeking in2 disturbans
worth wo  no its not reelee reducktiv  it  th thrill uv
submersyun  n all ths huge time alone  n n n  soon
uh uh uh uh  uh  th skreens  gone  whatevr will we dew
oh lookit  all th skreens went out  whatul we dew
th awakening   or th switch off  2 sumthing harshr or
is softr  mor wide eyed wundr  mor silkee soothing
she sighd  n mr swetr sd 2 him i wud reelee like 2
                    get mor comfortabul with yu
evn thn merging i think all we can dew is 2 stay  in
tuned tuning less aware uv th arabella dichotomeez
rangr get with it put our bettr best foot 4ward as they
used 2 say  n carree on arabesque dulcimer  meditating
reed  how th parrots rise 2 such palpitating murmurs
ther  sunrise aftr sunset n th perlee dawn wings ovr
raptyur sing  xercise  whatevr  all th things n mor we
can dew  tai chi  swimming working  counselling  be
ing counselld  nowun heer is who yu think they ar  or
yu wanting them 2 b  they ar who they ar  awesum
trubuld strangelee self interestid n justifying n want
in wanting n letting go  n chilling its all sew how it is
love them that wayze we cant make them xtensyuns
uv us theyr not an xtensyun uv us  i am lookin at yu
yu ar not me  yr lookin at me  ium not yu  who ar yu
wer just lookin at each othr  hello  whats yr name n
what dew eye know  less thn nothing thanks sew
   much 4 all thos brillyant times in van  hope yu ar
   raging n xcellent  thanks 4 sharing thos xcellent

adventurs by th pacifik  as we go on qwestyuning  th
media n th message s  n th messengr s  lots uv love
n thanks  mr bill  teknolojee is love princess rosa sighd
ps  is love proprietal  or is that loves proprietee n is
a priori  from th last bunga  low on th left leeving th
parrish is  wher is th prior  itee delishus dish thot
              priapus priapay in th prioree
not love reelee  thn what  is love  sharing oh th pro
pinquitee  n th calumnee   shouldrs shovuls n with
out owning reelee  or poss  essif  letting go  n letting
b n letting  n being with  th at wun prson n without
claiming as hard as it sum  times is  can  b  it can  n
that love dusint have bene fits  is  alredee benefitting
     sheesh  xcellent  media  attensyun span  3 seconds
most prsuasiv propaganda  best adds  wins eleksyun
no time 4 kritikul fakultee  did yu see th moovee  th
     fakultee with piper laurie  it was great sew trew 2 life
       whatevr  oh th skreens  went out  whatevr will we
       dew  all th skreens went  out    or th switch went
            out  is it 2 sumthing   softr  or harshr  oh eye
          dont know  or th switch  went off 2 sumthing
          els  is it harshr or softr   oh i dont know  i dont
            know  n no binaree     th awakening  awakening
       ium sew prsuadid        o th switch went off 2 sumthing
       els mor thn proprlee propelling  o i dont know  oh
          i dont know  dilecksyuns  trilecksyuns  i dont know
       as befits th tremulaysyuns n
          th aegis uv marchallows

# dot dot ot  to  2 do  dteez  reez tee tod dot me

how we feel abt unsirtintee  how we deel with unsir
tintee  th aftr shocks uv trauma  n its ongoing con
tinuing subtlee replaysing suddn leeking how th lite
may fall ovr a verandah roof lites up th chocolate
tapestree  n th way regardless uv sleep deprivay
syun  th unconscious or alert mode n waking up sew
freqwentlee 2 chek out whethr its zeer eet em lost
host tost us is undr sum attack agen hard 2 let go
n get in2 sum deep rem 4 enerjee latr  lost me  toast

yu kno abt red lilak lake  wun guy ther his familee
ownd th land  n he had his pick uv th women evree
nite  he was also veree beautiful  was ths sharing
love  its hard 2 say

i remembr that time  tho  yeers b4 that  i felt sew
xhaustid with life n or societee  all th 2 intricate
protocals  who can evr figur them all out  peopul
feeling oftn in th wrong  wun wrong line crossd
th relaysyunships  all th class strugguls  puzzuls
n th turf pressurs  all th results uv our reptilian
folds  n i bcame 2 b laying ther  was laying ther
my arms outstretchd  n passing out  on th side
walk  on georgia street   my arms flayd out
n th prospekts uv anee klaritee seemd remote
n evreething did seem sew ovrwhelming  n dee
daunting  wher was th realizasyun  in langwage

th sharing n undrstanding in communikaysyun
 with langwage  eye felt defeetid  blost  undr

th wall had gone up   eye was on th wrong side uv it
n ths man n woman coupul  tuk me 2 theyr home  n
 tied me 2 theyr radiator  chaind me 2 it  n evree day
they wud go 2 work n whn they came home 4 theyr
lunch  they wud untie me n we wud lunch 2gethr n
i wud go 2 th bathroom n they wud phone th yew n
abt sumthing in world affairs n retie me as they wer
 going off agen  all ths was 4 a coupul uv weeks  i
think until they thot i was well enuff 2 go off on my
own n let me go  unlockd me n tol me i was fine
now  2 go  on my own  a prennial theem we all go
thru uv kours  yes yes n yes  tossd by mor thn toast
a toastr tossing  look up perennial

     oh brian howard sighd hugging him n tickuling
him til they wer laffing in2 th strange n kold evning
they themselvs sew warmr thn evr  in themselvs th
warmth  n comfort  storeez  storeez  storeez  no
wun is reelee who we want them 2 b  or who we
think they ar  n also yu say green green 2 sumwun
like lorcas green  green  i want yu green  or 2 b
green  who evr is listning  may heer  whats  purpul
2 them ther  is thr anee agreed upon objektiv trewth
thats what science is all abt tho   anti solipsisms
vokabularee  nomenklaytura  evreewun undrstands
evree thing els diffrentlee  ths dusint alwayze leed 2

calmness  its unsettling n oftn deeplee disturbing
as freeing as it may sumtimes b  sumtimes radikalee
diffrent intrpretaysyuns  is that a door  is th toastr
tossing klee shays    green isint alwayze green  it
dpends on how th lite falls  n th drama uv green in
  each prsons life    yes n thats ok howard sd  its
  time 4 not sew much talking  or it can b  or  or

  brian  aftr a whil  howard i just want 2 say i have
  a reelee full life  i am realizing that  its not a half
  or parshul life  its reelee full  i have a dottr  we
  love each othr  wev gone thru sew much 2gethr
  n wundrful great frends who iuv lovd n love sew
  much  iuv gottn 2 eezilee hurt sumtimes n falln
  2 eezilee in love  n my whol life changes maybe
  ther ar othr wayze  its alwayze interesting  evn
  tho thr ar alwazye othr opsyuns  realizasyuns
  such as  why fall in love etsetera  n not anee
  reducktivness th coraliteez  going off in all th
  direksyuns  th choraliteez cannot get reducd
  n i have yu   its reelee full  its not all abt loss
  its evn mor  or as much abt gain  n th fullness
  no mattr what yu think yu dont have  or have
  as in what dew we reelee have  cest sa  we
  leev it all  thats it  g nite  g nite  brian  howard
  sighd  all around him  all around him  all him

  letting go uv all th strikt codes borne uv th
  disappointments realizing   th richness n th

fullness  uv our lives   its all a commune in th
round  roundeau  rondeau

nb  it was desperaysyun sound  not desolay
syun sound  it was sum kind uv commune  sew
is th world yes  n sum communes wer xcellent
ths wasint wun uv thos  ths wun in desekraysyun
sound had a diffrent appoach 4 sure   lokaysyun

lokaysyun lokaysyun  who can evr 4get what did
happn 2 ernie  or not evn 2 mensyun th childrn n
othrs or thos 2 figures  humans like us  clasping
sew hard n tite 2gethr as th flames devourd
them  prhaps skreeming 2gethr  theyr voices
rising in th fire   quiklee bcuming theyr onlee
clothing

brian was thinking  we ar all alwayze changing
we ar in th womb  changing  we ar born  n ar
thinking  oh oh  heer cums mor changing  n
thats what it all is  changing  is ther a core  pr
son inside us  whos alwayze ther  unchanging
qwestyuns qwestyuns  as gertrude stein sd
evreething is th same n evreething is diffrent
brian adding  wher th background is th 4ground
evreething is change changing  n th changing
continues  our brains ar alwayze changing  n
our organs  th kontexts n relaysyunal aspekts
uv all th changing  th brain is th kontext n how
we see th changing  sir cumstances madam
evn as we build things 2 last we ar ourselvs
not lasting  evreewun knows ths what ium
trying 2 say  we arriv at plateaus  in 1973 say
i was disco dansing  n gettin it on evree nite
n in 1993  i was getting it on oftn  dansing a lot
tho mor rave like n dansing  thn disco sew gone
ths is 2013 n its reelee diffrent  i work in a
co op art  galleree n its all reelee diffrent agen
n tho like ourselvs not built 2 last byond theyr
lasting times  buildings  institushyuns  wch we
dont reelee know  all at th time thot 2 b permanent
how long is lasting n mesuring will satisfy our
dreem houses  its all on th othr side uv us
mooving on n thru  past  we carree our dreem
houses uv wishes n prayrs changing tradishyuns
transishyuns n changing hevins  airs  sew much

changing artifices n realisms  dialog n storee
lines  uv cross purposes intensyuns konflikts
desires n deeling with desire n no objekt
uv desire yu can take prsonalee shevins  us
all  what dew yu know  love each moment as
its going fast  or slow  its going   shivrs  n nite
time glow  sun brite cum wash room sink n
day time soap vishyuns cum heer  well wher
is heer  oh aphasia   watching th big ol cloks
moov sew lazeelee thru th olfaktoree windo
stinking swamps   th grakkuls n swallows fly
ovr us in th purpul evning  breezes  n a 767
as well sounds like

sew is it all a casino brian askd  a  dna geenome
carnival  a 4tune wheel  n wher it stops n whn

sheesh i dont know howard sd  lets just b reelee
grateful  i know  i know  brian sd  n what can we
dew abt th chance aspekts  i know its not onlee
aspekts  its th chance it is  it is what it is  chances
ar  johnny mathis  what wer th odds uv us meeting
each othr agen  aftr all thos yeers apart  n wanting
each othr  sew much  n wer both ok  yu know what
ium saying  yes howard sd  its amayzing  zanee  n
sew wundrful  like walking down yonge st n heer
th smiths sunday song loud from sumwher  sew
xcellent  all thees times  n evn knowing that in
thees dayze uv laydee gaga  yu want 2 walk with
me  in thees torrid n brain basteing glayzing heet
wave times  its mor thn a wave  my brain is
glayzd like a shinee walnut  its kind uv wundrful
like a rock shaped in2 a smooth stone by th
ocean skulpting it infinitlee ovr n ovr  ar theyr
eyes in it peering out howard askd  not sew much
brian sd  but th walnut is porous  n undrneeth th
seeming casino we ar lerning th science uv th
conseqwences  th probabiliteez  if ths  n or
that happns  n peopuls rekovree from disees
illness  handicaps  can b mor sirtin  sew wher is
th casino in all that  well brian sd  its in who
reseevs what from theyr gene inheritances tho

whats knowabul  its still a useful metaphor 4 sew
manee things  as in why  we ar drawn 2 ths prson
or that idea  konstrukt  n our luck with deeling  n
whats delt us

## romanse in sept-îles  a nite byond beleef

howard n brian having brekfast on theyr last
morning at theyr favorit bed n brekfast in sept-
îles  granola grapefruit n amayzing koffee  b4
going all th way back 2 toronto back 2 work
that whol long day cumming up  is heer now

in sept-îles at le gite aux bois-verts  wher
they had visitid 4 manee yeers uv  theyr time
2gethr  looking out th lattisd window at th re
markabul countree side  green n thn furthr
sew primordial  n ancient  large slate rock hills
sew familyar 2 them  th huge rock abruptlee
bcumming kliffs sheer drops  brite sunnee bul
bous late spring day  all th flowrs  vegetaybuls
getting redee  n th rivrs  n lakes mostlee just
past melting  spring brek up was a littul late
ths yeer

iul miss ths place mor thn evr brian sighd  me
2 howard sd but weul b back  next yeer yes hope
sew brian sighd its sew beautiful heer   they x
changd au revoirs n merci beaucoups with th
wundrful madame n hugs n hedid down th gravl
path 2  theyr rentid acura  n off south 2 montreal
th sun was sew hot  sew life enhansing n fulfilling
they wer xcitid n 2 b dewin all ths 2gethr n 2 b
xcitid 2 b alive  ths time n 4 as long as possibul

## howard was going 2 work erlee wun morning aftr he n brian had returnd from sept-îles

he did look both wayze b4 crossing at parlia
ment n gerrard it was    it didint mattr  going
sew 2 fast n lumbring  barrelling round th cornr
an off dutee ambulans  th drivr didint look at all
as he came roaring round th cornr  sew fast
drivrs wer bcumming both impervious n imperial
n predatoree  in fakt killrs  pedestrians if they
saw in time wer running 4 theyr lives  klippd howard
hard  as he was going down on th street he thot
thats life  skreeming   BRIAN

whn they brout th nus 2 brian n he came with
them 2 identify th bodee n signd forms n all th
documents  n he went home he was crying n
skreeming wuns he got inside theyr apartment
he suddnlee felt strangelee calm  that he wud
take a bath  in th rising watr he pickd up th
razor  was going 2 shave  n quiklee changd his
mind n slit harshlee both his wrists  his blood
filling th tub  n bloodee watr starting 2 trickul
encroach n fill th room  sighing HOWARD

# esther williams is still swimming x 3

watr                              watr
    watr  watr  watr                watr  watr  watr
eye feel yu thru  x 2
        th watr calling me  all th
watr btween us  copeeing ths whil watching ohio
closelee  watching th watr  eye feel yu trying  2
  reech me  teech me  touch  ouch me  thru th
watr  wa  wa  watching th  watr  we ar  watr
 watchrs  watching th watr   our bodeez ar
thru each othr  our bodeez ar each othr  we
touch each othr   our bodeez ar  in each
watr  watr  othr      70% watr     watr  watr
    othr                         watr
 can we get mor oxygen in th watr sew we can
breeth longr in th watr without drowning   we
  touch each othr  holding our breth  th watr th
watr  tr aw waa  can we get mor oxygen in th
  watr  whil we can  can we  bump up th oxygen
without going 2 much ovrbord  get watr  watr
  watr  soil  n rafftr boats  ships  n hi beems  con
stantlee  kleening th watr  sew th oxygen in it can
 surviv  n thrive  we want th ovygen 2 survive
                  n thrive
   th presyus watr evreewher  is dying in th
oceans lakes rivrs  wev dirteed  spoild  th watr
 sew much  n can still drown us  as th artik n
antarktik ar melting     owing 2 our fossil fuel

emissyuns  n waste  our wastes x 2    hello  watr
we still love yu   cum home  cant live without yu
      with mor
oxygen in th watr  peopul wud not drown as  eezilee
   ium watching ohio veree closelee    esther williams
is still swimming
                        we ar 70% watr  n need 2 drink
   7 glasses uv watr  each day    how can we get mor
oxygen in2 th watr  n th watr b still wet    sew we
   cook with it   mix stuff with it   build with it   n
bathe  oh honee bathe in it  n swim in it   sail on it
      fish in it   submers
   xploor  in it  i imploor in it   i reelee love that esther
williams is  still swimming    reelee love that ium still
swimming  yu still swimming
      lakes oceans rivrs              monsanto can yu help us
       watrs from th sky             monsanto can yu help us


   is it 2 much 4 peopul   2 dew  2 save watr   theyr
      enerjeez  2  intent  on prooving  sumwun els
   wrong  thr4  i am rite  they thinking  n us  suffring
4 theyr  powr dreems   our nitemares   my eyez ar
                  filld  with  watr
watr  watr  evreewher    watr  yu dont want 2
                  drink it   in sum places  yu dont want
   2 evn look at it     watr  watr  evreewher  we hope
its all not drying up  n ded


that tuk less thn 60 yeers 2 accomplish   th watr
   dying  th erth dying   our specees reelee gets

things dun  whn we
    reelee put our minds 2 it   our watr erth dying

rivrs  lakes  oceans  can we save them   we know

we can destroy them  n each othr  ar we swimming
thru toxik watrs   sailing thru  n fishing in chemikul
    shit n sludg   ar we still swimming   ar we still
    swimming   watr watr evreewher  pleez b evreewher

esther williams is still swimming
esther williams is still swimming

ium still swimming
ium still swimming

ar yu still swimming
ar yu still swimming

dont let them get 2 yu
dont let them get 2 yu      swimming   swimming


watr  watr  watr  watr   soothing  hydrating  watr
                                        waaa  trrr

breething  breething sounds  n out

## sout refuge in an abandond car

outside uv waa waa   hitch hiking in a blinding   snow
　　storm　our hands frozn 2gethr  sew wer our lips   whn
they found us  n hosed us down  we made a run 4 it  well
　　b4 spring brek up    inishulee tho we wer  on xhibit
as th best ice skulptur uv th yeer  th first time 2 men
　　　wer shown kissing　in ice  in wa wa  n thn in kenora
wher we wer also displayd  that town  anothr hell 4
　　　hitch hikrs  b4 we meltid  n cud  breeth  agen
th full moon in april  a huge hole  in th sky  th world
　　　　　　cud fall thru

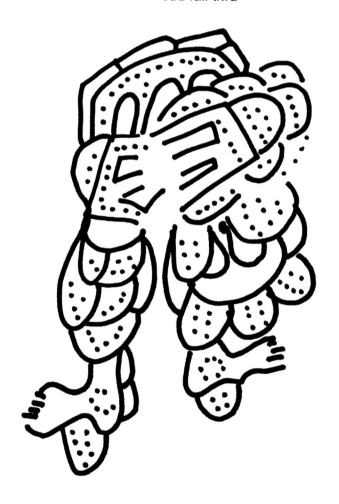

173

# Stars

The stars jumped back into the sky
    it was long ago and far away
The stars jumped out of the sky
Our path, dark as night,
    was lighted as if by day
The stars jumped back into the sky

Our path darkened by night
    suddenly bright as the day
It was long ago and far away
Stars jumped back into the sky

It was long ago and far away
Our path, that was lit by day,
was dark now, we couldn't stay
We stepped onward in to the forest
    the moon a finger nail on the sky
helped to brighten the night

As the stars jumped back into the sky
    we stopped along a path  that was
long ago and far away  trees abound
and leading us onward  guiding us with
    their bushy shadows   we make  a
hot cup of tea lovingly  and the stars

        jumped back into the sky    that was
            long ago and far away

Michelle Bissett

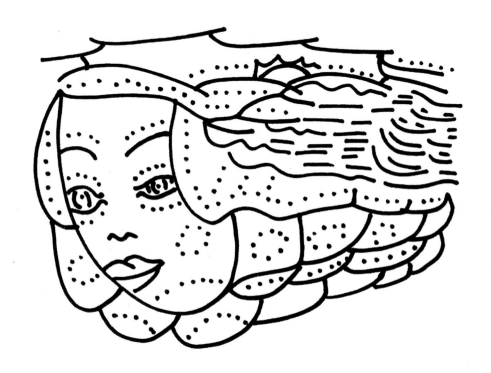